**Other Works by William S. Burroughs
Published by Grove Press**

Junky: The Definitive Text of "Junk"

Nova Express: The Restored Text

Naked Lunch: The Restored Text

The Soft Machine: The Restored Text

The Ticket That Exploded: The Restored Text

The Adding Machine: Selected Essays

The Wild Boys: A Book of the Dead

Word Virus: The William S. Burroughs Reader

And The Hippos Were Boiled in Their Tanks: A Novel
(with Jack Kerouac)

Last Words: The Final Journals of William Burroughs

QUEER

WILLIAM S. BURROUGHS

EDITED AND WITH
AN INTRODUCTION
BY OLIVER HARRIS

Grove Press

New York

First published in 1985 in the United States of America by Viking Penguin Inc.
This expanded edition was first published in 2010 by Penguin Books.

First Grove Atlantic paperback edition: September 2022

Simultaneously published in Canada
Printed in Canada

ISBN 978-0-8021-6056-0
eISBN 978-0-8021-6057-7

Library of Congress Cataloging-in-Publication data is available for this title.

Grove Press
an imprint of Grove Atlantic
154 West 14th Street
New York, NY 10011

Distributed by Publishers Group West

groveatlantic.com

23 24 25 26   10 9 8 7 6 5 4 3 2

CONTENTS

ACKNOWLEDGMENTS

I would like to thank James Grauerholz for his scholarly expertise and generous support on this project and over the past twenty-five years of friendship and collaboration. I would also like to thank Erling Wold for sharing his understanding of *Queer*, Keith Seward for his comments on the introduction, Paul Slovak and the team at Penguin, and Jeffrey Posternak at the Wylie Agency.

For their personal assistance with manuscript research, I would like to thank Isaac Gewirtz, curator of the Henry W. and Albert A. Berg Collection of English and American Literature, New York Public Library; Michael Ryan, Gerald Cloud, and Jennifer Lee of the Rare Book and Manuscript Library, Columbia University; and Polly Armstrong and Mattie Taormina of the Department of Special Collections at Green Library, Stanford University.

I also gratefully acknowledge the David Bruce Centre for American Studies at Keele University and the British Academy for financially supporting my research. I dedicate this 2022 edition to Stacie, for being there.

"The Appalling Conclusion"

T he morning Jack Kerouac arrived at 210 Calle Oriz-
aba, the first Saturday of May 1952, the señoras in the street
were cooking up tortillas and the radio was playing Perez
Prado. The big-band sound of the Mambo King from
Cuba, lately dubbed the Glenn Miller of Mexico, was iron-
ically bland mood music for what Kerouac found in apartment number 5, his old friend William Burroughs appearing
to him that May morning "like a mad genius in littered
rooms": "He was writing. He looked wild, but his eyes innocent and blue and beautiful."[1] Kerouac's double take, his
contrary image of Burroughs as a crazed madman amid
chaos yet also a figure of startling purity, is a precise match
for the "simultaneous double exposure" of Burroughs' self-
portraits in the novel whose writing Kerouac interrupted—
"The face was ravaged and vicious and old," we are told of
William Lee; the "eyes were dreamy and innocent"—while
suggesting both the paradoxical nature of that novel and
the circumstances in which he wrote it.

Since there are no "straight" books in the William
Burroughs oeuvre—any one of them might be called *Queer*—
his second novel is perversely typical and fulfills the meaning

of the title as noun (homosexual—used pejoratively or with pride), adjective (peculiar, false, dubious), and verb (to thwart, unnerve, unsettle). Certainly, from its writing in 1952 to its eventual publication in 1985 and its reputation twenty-five years on, everything about *Queer* is perplexing. It is unflinchingly personal but also coruscatingly political, a seemingly realist narrative that breaks into the wildest fantasies, with material in it of such undecided tone that it's hard to know whether to howl with laughter or dismay. A genuinely queer fish, it is at one and the same time a book of revelations and an inscrutable text, an early autobiographical embarrassment that Burroughs abandoned incomplete and a secret he left buried for three decades, both a botched job and a taste of things to come—the piquant appetizer to the nauseating *Naked Lunch*. Queer indeed.

Why *Queer* differs so dramatically from *Junky*, the debut novel Burroughs wrote immediately before it (published in 1953 as *Junkie*), and why it did not appear in print for more than thirty years; where it stands in his literary development and how it fits into a history of homosexual writing; and why it is simultaneously unique in Burroughs' work for its dramatization of desire and yet best known for a death it does not even describe—these are among the riddles it poses. Setting the historical record straight is all the trickier because, in effect, there is not one *Queer* but two—the manuscript Burroughs wrote in 1952 and the book that was published thirty-three years later. This new edition works with both texts to re-present *Queer*, on its twenty-fifth anniversary, with the hope of grasping this slim but slippery novel and revealing it in a fresh light.

Kerouac's vivid description of Burroughs in early May 1952 captures the acute ambiguity of his situation. On the one hand, just a month earlier Ace Books had formally agreed to accept Burroughs' first novel, then still titled "Junk," and he was, at age thirty-eight, for the first time self-consciously anticipating a literary future. With undisguised delight, Burroughs' letters that April suddenly begin to speak of "we authors" and "us writers," and he tells Allen Ginsberg, then acting as his literary agent, to save his letters for "a book of them later on when I have a rep."[2] Note "when," rather than *if.* . . . On the other hand, every letter Burroughs wrote that year used a false name on the envelope in order to escape the prying eyes of Mexican officials—because Kerouac's intrusion on the writing of *Queer* followed only eight months after that fateful evening when Burroughs' Star .380 automatic shot low and put a bullet through the forehead of his wife, the glass he was aiming at rolling unbroken along the floor near a table with four empty bottles of Oso Negro gin. That drunken act of madness would cast a long, dark shadow over whatever writing success Burroughs might have in Mexico, South America, Tangier, Paris, London, New York, or his final home in Lawrence, Kansas.

The shooting of Joan Vollmer has loomed large in the legend of Burroughs and the Beat circle for obvious reasons, but the pairing of her death with his second novel only came about in 1985, due to lines that are quoted as often as anything he ever wrote: "the book is motivated and formed by an event which is never mentioned, in fact is carefully avoided: the accidental shooting death of my wife, Joan, in September 1951," and "I am forced to the appalling conclusion that I would never have become a writer but for Joan's death." Made all the more stunning by Burroughs' reluctance to speak frankly about it over the years, these lines from his 1985 introduction to *Queer* (see appendix) put the novel in the spotlight's glare. As a traumatic report of the real, his revelation also had the perverse effect of framing the text with such a sensational context that it all but obscured both the fiction itself and any other reality behind it.

That gunshot was the turning point in Burroughs' life, and *Queer* was an equally decisive turning point in Burroughs' writing, but it is possible, in fact necessary, to separate the two. First, it is simply not the case that Joan's death is "carefully avoided" in *Queer*: in terms of its fictionalization of autobiographical events, the shooting falls outside the narrative chronology, which ends in late summer 1951. Without Burroughs' introduction, few would have thought to make the connection. Further, Burroughs offered an entirely distinct explanation for why, even though they were written back-to-back, his second novel differed so radically from his first—why only in *Queer* do we find the trademark comic-grotesque turns that would take center stage in *Naked Lunch*. "The difference of course is simple," he explains: *Junky* is a novel of addiction, *Queer* a novel of withdrawal, and "during withdrawal he may feel the compulsive need for an audience, and this is clearly what Lee seeks. . . . So he invents a frantic attention-getting format which he calls the Routine." The simplicity of this explanation is complicated by Burroughs' curious refusal to distinguish between himself and his persona, or between the events of 1951 and their fictionalization in 1952, but this account at least has the advantage of being precise in relation to the subject of his two novels and in line with how he saw them at the time of writing.

"The Special Chaos of a Dream"

Having moved his family—his wife, Joan; her daughter, Julie; and their son, Billy—from South Texas to Mexico City in the fall of 1949, Burroughs started writing "Junk" in early 1950 and by the end of the year had completed a first-draft manuscript (on which he continued to work during the next two years). When, in late March 1952, he reported beginning its as-yet-untitled sequel, Burroughs described to Kerouac the major difference—the shift from first- to third-person narration—in these terms: "Part I is on the junk, Part II off." If we see *Junky* and *Queer* as consecutive chapters in Burroughs' life, each documenting one of his outlaw demimonde identities, this might be enough to explain why in the first novel William Lee is cool and detached, his narration of events factual and dryly ironic, while in the second Lee is "disintegrated," as Burroughs put it in his 1985 introduction, "desperately in need of contact, completely unsure of himself and of his purpose." But it also seems to muddle up the written with the circumstances of writing—Burroughs was actually back on the junk the whole time he worked on *Queer*—and fails to explain the rapid disintegration of the novel itself. For

Queer starts out, like *Junky*, with the realist documentation of a social scene—"The bearded set never frequented the Ship Ahoy" is a direct parallel to "The hipster-bebop junkies never showed at 103rd Street"—only to break down, collapse into episodic fragments and disjointed fantasies, and then, abruptly, stop.

In fact, the seeds of disintegration are there from the opening line. Burroughs begins without warning in medias res ("Lee turned his attention to a Jewish boy named Carl Steinberg") and quickly confuses both national identity ("Born in Munich, Carl had grown up in Baltimore") and the very location of the narrative, since it's not at all clear that the setting is Mexico City: the "Amsterdam Avenue park" Lee walks through not only names a city in Holland but for many North American readers probably suggests the Upper West Side of Manhattan. The fact that Burroughs is describing the Parque México, around which runs the oval-shaped Calle Amsterdam, does nothing to buttress an appearance of solid realism, however, since Lee promptly seats himself on "a concrete bench that was molded to resemble wood"—an improbably surreal piece of furniture, notwithstanding the fact that such benches really do exist in the Parque México.[3]

These first pages merely set the scene, and hint at the baffling difference between the representation of biographically real people and places here and in *Junky*. To identify Hal Chase behind Winston Moor or Frank Jeffries behind Tom Williams, or to say that Lola's was actually Tato's Bar, adjacent to Mexico City College at 154 San Luis Potosí, or that the Ship Ahoy was really the Bounty Bar and Grill on the corner of Monterrey and Chihuahua, and below the apartment in which the shooting of Joan took place—such source-hunting tells us very little about *Queer*. The point about the Rathskeller where Lee meets Moor is not that its cuckoo clocks confirm it was modeled on the Ku Ku Restaurant on Calle Coahuila and Avenida de los Insurgentes (Burroughs actually typed "KuKu clocks" in his manuscript) but that they and the "moth-eaten deer heads" give it an "out-of-place, Tyrolean look"—and that this odd displacement typifies the representation of place, and people, in *Queer*.

For a short book initially set in one small part of a single city, it has a remarkably large and chaotic cast of characters and places from elsewhere, with references to Oklahoma City, Uruguay, Salt Lake City, Zihuatanejo, Frankfurt, the Tex-Mex border, Dallas, Peru, Russia, Scotland, Cuba, the Amazon, Rome, Alaska, Veracruz, Baghdad, Prague, the Upper Ubangi, Tanhajaro, the Zambesi, Timbuktu, Dakar, Marrakesh, Morelia, Bogotá, Barcelona, Poland, Budapest, Tibet, Canada, and so on. Never eating Mexican food, Lee dines at the American K.C. Steak House, a Russian restaurant, and then a Chinese one, and when he goes to the movies, it's to see a French film based on a Greek myth (Cocteau's *Orphée*). And so, while Jorge García-Robles is absolutely correct to say that "if there exists a 'Mexican novel' in the Burroughs oeuvre, it is *Queer*,"[4] this is to miss the point just as much as it would be to say how little Burroughs seems to have engaged with Mexico and its culture. The one literary reference, to the Irish author Frank Harris, only underscores the point.

"Mexico is sinister and gloomy and chaotic with the special chaos of a dream," Burroughs had informed Kerouac in May 1951, and the Mexico City of *Queer* is not a "realist" city at all. The Cuba, a bar "with an interior like the set for a surrealist ballet" that features androgynous mermaids and "disquieting" fish, sums up the feeling that there is indeed something disquietingly surreal and fishy beneath *Queer*'s outward realism. When Lee and his reluctant lover, Allerton, reach Ecuador, the dream dimension becomes overpowering, immediately fulfilling the "nightmare undercurrent" in Lee's account of taking peyote by revealing "some undercurrent of life that was hidden from him." The rivers here contain "nameless monsters" that in turn echo the "nameless obscenities" decorating ancient Chimu pottery, the very repetition of the phrases suggesting that this dreadful place, "The Land Where Anything Goes" ("Men changing into huge centipedes"), is a terrain where inner horrors are acted out. The monstrous landscape of South America grows out of earlier metaphysical disturbances, as when Lee appears "curiously spectral, as though you could see through his face," or Winston Moor gives off "a faint, greenish steam of decay," or Allerton talks in the "eerie, disembodied voice of a young child" and Lee reaches out toward him with "ectoplasmic fingers" and "phantom thumbs."

If the realist narrative seems to fall apart and be metaphorically all over the place, so too is William Lee, who, like some overwound mechanical talking toy, repeats the same jokes, either verbatim ("Sit down on your ass, or what's left of it after four years in the navy") or with small variations. The flat, bare narrative is overwhelmed by Lee's ever-more-extreme tall tales but so too is Lee himself, as the line between putting on voices and being possessed by them breaks down. Rather than trying to entertain and seduce Allerton with his stories, Lee is left literally speaking in tongues, his longest routine "coming to him like dictation" and carrying on without any audience at all. Lee is breaking down because his desire for Allerton literally tears him apart. *Queer* is accordingly saturated with Lee's fantasies of bodily merger and recurrent images of pain and amputation. Although the parallels with the myth of Orpheus are inviting—in Ovid's version (but not Cocteau's), the poet is torn to pieces because, after the death of his wife, Eurydice, he gives up the love of women for the pursuit of boys—the parallel between Lee's fate and Burroughs' narrative demonstrates the increasingly destabilizing force of desire at the level of the writing itself.

Burroughs himself seemed blind to the contradiction of planning to write, as he put it to Kerouac in late March 1952, "a queer novel using the same straight narrative method as I used in *Junk*." You might say that in its very failure to sustain a "straight narrative method" *Queer* became itself, and described like this, we can also begin to see how its failures predicted Burroughs' greatest success. That is to say, from one point of view, *Queer* is not novelistic enough, but from the perspective of where Burroughs was heading—the chaotic mosaic of *Naked Lunch* (1959)—it was the narrative form itself that, in 1952, held the writing back. In some ways, *Queer* is more haunting and unnerving than *Naked Lunch*, where the satirical intent is clear and the reader is lost inside Burroughs' darkest imaginings, rather than made a horrified witness to his alter ego's excruciating psychic collapse. The origins of *Naked Lunch* in the cracking up of *Queer* appear quite literally at the moment when Lee first attempts to court Allerton with a friendly greeting and "there emerged instead a leer of naked lust, wrenched in the pain and hate of his deprived body and, in simultaneous double exposure, a sweet child's smile of liking and trust, shockingly out of time and place, mutilated and hopeless." By an accident that was no accident at all, a misreading of Lee's "naked lust" in the manuscript of *Queer* would, in 1953, give Burroughs the title *Naked Lunch*.[5] But if the breakdown of *Queer* anticipates the breakthrough of Burroughs' masterpiece, then reciprocally, and despite its reputation as a drug book, we can also better recognize the queerness of *Naked Lunch*, which was written—like *Queer*—out of desire as much as on drugs. But this is to get ahead of ourselves, and we should remember that in the spring of 1952 Burroughs was sharing his apartment with Jack Kerouac, since the rendezvous of the two writers reveals a good deal about the forces that both drove and disrupted Burroughs' novel.

Writing to Ginsberg on May 10, Kerouac reported that, having found a new typewriter, he and Burroughs had "resumed work on our respective books"—meaning *Queer* (a title Kerouac had suggested to Burroughs before arriving in Mexico) and *Doctor Sax*.[6] That Kerouac wrote *Sax* during his two-month stay with Burroughs is well known, but what's been overlooked is the profound and precise influence the writers had on each other during this crucial period in their careers. Kerouac's novel reveals multiple traces—in theme, allusion, and specific phrasings—of his reading of Burroughs' manuscript.[7] Burroughs, for his part, reported to Ginsberg in mid-May that Kerouac "has developed unbelievably," and while it's unclear whether Burroughs read any of *Doctor Sax*, we do know that he had been reading, and was "very much impressed by," the just-finished manuscript Kerouac brought with him to Mexico: *Visions of Cody*. Indeed, back in April Burroughs had seen excerpts and compared them to Joyce's *Finnegans Wake*. This was an apt comparison because Kerouac was at this time at the very height of his powers and confidence as an experimental writer. It was during May 1952 that he first defined his "sketching" technique (later formalized as "spontaneous prose") and by early June—inspired after listening with Burroughs to jazz records by Stan Getz, Charlie Parker, and Miles Davis—had come up with the term "wild form" to describe his own jazzy methods of improvisational composition and performative storytelling. It's possible that Kerouac's passion for experimenting with form in *Cody* and *Sax* had an influence on *Queer*. At the very least, it might have led Burroughs to worry less about the unstable roughness of his own new manuscript. Then again, it's the differences between the two writers that tell us most about *Queer*.

In mid-May, Kerouac had described his spontaneous methods of writing as the perfect medium, telling Ginsberg that sketching "never fails, it's the thing itself."[8] When Burroughs wrote Ginsberg a week later, it was to describe his work in progress in fundamentally different terms:

"Writing must always remain an *attempt*. The Thing itself, the process on sub-verbal level always eludes the writer. A medium suitable for me does not yet exist, unless I invent it." Initially, *Queer* had followed the autobiographical narrative and "factualist" template of *Junky*. But the difference between need, which can be fulfilled or "fixed," in the junkie's sense, and desire, which is always an attempt doomed to fail (Lee "felt the tearing ache of limitless desire"), determined why a "straight" method, a factualist straitjacket, would not work for *Queer*. Reversing his own account of the shift from *Junky* to *Queer*, it would be truer to say that Burroughs wrote Part I "off" desire, Part II on.

"A Kind of Field-Trip in Sociology"

If the clash between "queer" subject and "straight" method escaped his attention at the time, the queerest thing about Burroughs' introduction, written three decades later, is his reluctance to see *Queer* as a "queer novel" at all. Although he experienced homosexual desire long before he became a drug addict, the belated publication of his second novel did nothing to put Burroughs' identity as a queer on a par with that as a junky. It may have been an act of diplomacy on his part not to reveal the autobiographical reality behind William Lee's courtship of Gene Allerton—his own pursuit of Lewis Marker, a twenty-one-year-old student at Mexico City College—but, still, Burroughs' insistence that Lee was "not really looking for sex contact" and that it "had

nothing to do with Allerton as a character" strangely cuts
off the story from its historical basis. And yet from the
start, from the first time he mentioned writing it to Ginsberg, Burroughs framed his novel in this context, not only
identifying that sexual relationship as its "central theme,"
but discussing Donald Webster Cory's recently published
The Homosexual in America (1951). After Alfred Kinsey's
sensational *Sexual Behavior in the Human Male* (1948),
Cory's book was the most influential study of the subject
and offers a precise context for considering the queerness
of Burroughs' second novel.

The Homosexual in America advanced a political position that Burroughs derided in his letter to Ginsberg. But
what he does not mention is that it also made the case for
a gay literary tradition, and since *Queer* was about to add to
it, Burroughs must surely have read Cory's discussion with
interest. Going back to the start of literary history, Cory
observes that "*The Satyricon* of Petronius is the oldest
extant novel," and that "this gives the homosexual the
distinction of being the protagonist in the first novel to
survive the passage of time."[9] Burroughs never made the
connection in quite this way, but it is no coincidence that
in later years he would often identify his 1950s trilogy—
Junky, *Queer*, and *The Yage Letters* (1963)—with the pica-
resque tradition and date it back to Petronius. More
immediately, it's striking how little Burroughs had to say
about the contemporary literary context established by
Cory.

In his letters at the time of writing *Queer*, Burroughs
makes passing references to Jean Genet and Gore Vidal,

while in the prologue to *Junky*, also written in the summer of 1952, he lists Gide and Wilde among his adolescent reading. But his brief discussion in early April of Vidal's recently published *The Judgment of Paris* gives no hint that Burroughs had found anything of interest in Vidal's more notorious novel of homosexual experience, *The City and the Pillar* (1948).[10] Then again, *The City and the Pillar* has its place alongside other postwar novels such as James Barr's *Quatrefoil* (1950) and Fritz Peters' excellent *Finistère* (1951)—both discussed by Cory—in a gay literary tradition that *Queer* simply doesn't fit into. Nor does it seem useful to make comparisons with Isherwood's Berlin stories or those of Firbank, or with Carson McCullers' *Reflections in a Golden Eye* (1942), Capote's *Other Voices, Other Rooms* (1948), or John Horne Burns' *The Gallery* (1947). Nor does it compare with the sexually explicit and intensely lyrical work of Genet (the subject in 1952 of Sartre's famous study *Saint Genet*). Djuna Barnes' *Nightwood* (1936)—much admired by Burroughs—and *The Young and Evil* (1933) by Charles Henri Ford and Parker Tyler would have been of greater interest, but as much for their stylistic experiments as their sexual themes.[11] In fact, the most resonant connection for Burroughs in Cory's survey might well have been a book he had read in 1944 "to see what a drink cure is like": Charles Jackson's *The Lost Weekend*.[12]

Jackson's debut novel had been a national best seller in 1944, and in certain respects fictionally modeled Burroughs' own approach to the writing of *Junky*, if not *Queer*. Early on, Jackson's writer-protagonist, Don Birnam, visits a Greenwich Village bar like "a spectator making a kind of field-trip in sociology," savoring the sense that "he might have been invisible, the figure out of mythology."[13] Birnam's idea of objective literary research—paralleled in the novel's reception as a "case study"—approximates both Burroughs' own quasi-sociological approach to the writing of *Junky* and Lee's status as a virtually absent reporter, an *hombre invisible*. And the outcome of Birnam's visit— humiliation, when the acte gratuit of trying to steal a handbag is discovered—suggests both the ignominy of Burroughs' own failed criminal efforts and the masochism of his persona in *Queer*. The true relevance of Jackson's novel, however, lies in the fate that befell him in the wake of its success. Only a year after publication, *The Lost Weekend* became a Hollywood hit, sweeping the Oscars of 1945 and earning awards for director Billy Wilder and star Ray Milland. As with many other successful adaptations, the Hollywood version has all but taken the place of the literary original in the cultural memory. Few perhaps realize that the novel ends with Birnam entirely unrepentant and that his alcoholism was not an escape from writer's block; it was motivated by the trauma of repressed homosexuality.[14] Burroughs might have found the psychology in Jackson crude and the literary self-consciousness affected, but in Birnam's refusal of final moral redemption he might well have seen an inspiring example of defiance.

The censorship of *The Lost Weekend* was the beginning of the end for Jackson, however, whose second novel, *The Fall of Valor* (1946), was another case history but this time focused fully on the guilt of homosexual desire. The novel has not aged well, but its unpopularity in its own day measured the risks of a subject that no Hollywood ending could fix. In fact, the issue of how gay novels ended was one of Cory's central topics, and Burroughs must surely have thought about his discussion of the seemingly mandatory "tragic endings." Just three weeks after mentioning starting to write *Queer* and reading *The Homosexual in America*, he comments, "One thing, I have not decided on ending for second novel." Cory's book concluded that many homosexual writers purged themselves by inflicting "punishment upon their own *alter ego*," using "their books to 'cure' themselves of their guilt, and the reading audience becomes the unwitting confessor or the ill-paid analyst."[15] In the year that the American Psychiatric Association identified homosexuality as a mental illness (it would not be removed from its *Diagnostic and Statistical Manual of Mental Disorders* until twenty years later), this must have been a striking answer to the question Cory originally posed: "What role can a fictional portrait of homosexuality play?" Burroughs' own answer, and his sense of an ending, turned on his shifting understanding of what constituted the "reading audience" for his new work.

In March 1952, Burroughs' readership seems to have been the pulp-paperback market identified with Ace Books; indeed, he felt *Queer* "is more saleable than *Junk*, and has a wider appeal. It is, in fact, more sensational." In later years, he would always claim that Ace rejected his second novel because it turned out to be *too* sensational: "They said I'd be in jail if I published it."[16] And while there's no supporting evidence for that claim, it goes without saying that the early 1950s was a dangerous time to publish a novel called

Queer. Although Burroughs rejected Cory's politics—and although Cory would have been appalled by Burroughs' novel—the politicization of the most private acts was the context that made Cory's book so timely in the first place.

"Imperious Desires"

This was not only the era of McCarthyism and the Korean War but the lavender scare, the Homintern conspiracy, and the demonization of homosexuality as an un-American, viral contagion and threat to the health of the body politic. A 1950 Senate report warned: "One homosexual can pollute a government office."[17] Lee observes that "they are purging the State Department of queers," and Burroughs could have found recent statistics set out for him in Cory's book (ninety-one dismissed, out of twenty-three thousand employees). He would also have found a politically sensitive study of homosexual idiom—including an appeal to replace terms like *fairy* and *fag* with *gay*—and Burroughs surely took note when Cory considers "the very impact of the words: *I am a homosexual, I am a queer, I am a fairy,*"[18] recording in *Queer* his own parodic version of the impact made by verbal labels: "when the baneful word seared my reeling brain: *homosexual.* I was a homosexual."

Burroughs mentioned none of this in his letter to Ginsberg, however, and instead lambasted Cory for his apparently liberal stand on tolerance: "Enough to turn a man's gut. This citizen says a queer learns humility, learns to turn the other cheek, and returns love for hate." In

Queer, Burroughs inverted the lesson and took his revenge on Cory by having Lee tell the story of Bobo, whose message of conquering "prejudice and ignorance and hate with knowledge and sincerity and love" is rewarded by literally having his guts torn out, Isadora Duncan–style: "riding in the Duc de Ventre's Hispano-Suiza when his falling piles blew out of the car and wrapped around the rear wheel." While Cory's political case advanced the homosexual's "solidarity" with "all the unfortunate, the despised, the oppressed of the earth," William Lee in *Queer* demonstrates the very opposite of such a "democratic spirit" among fellow victims.[19]

Despite *Queer*'s initial appearance, and reputation, as an intimately personal confession—"Burroughs's heart laid bare," according to Ginsberg's 1985 jacket blurb—its political stakes in the era of its writing are, by default, clarified by Cory's book. Burroughs' own 1985 introduction emphasized his private life at the expense of recalling that wider national history, but this is a historically false opposition, since it was precisely the politicization of the personal that defined cold war culture. This should prompt us to recognize not only how surprisingly dense Burroughs' queer novel is with political references but the connection it repeatedly implies between the intimate world of individual desires and a global narrative of power. Although Lee jokes that he has "not come to psychoanalyze Caesar," an analysis of empire is exactly what his story lays bare, most explicitly when he delivers a lecture that equates both sides of the cold war conflict with that essential Burroughs term, "Control.

The superego, the controlling agency, gone cancerous and berserk." The irony cuts both ways, for Lee's critique is truly self-lacerating given his own increasingly desperate fantasies of controlling Allerton, but the political point is that a queer—the most pathologically abject enemy within cold war America—should be diagnosing the imperial psyche of Washington. And Burroughs' queer is no mere gay with attitude: he's literally a gay with a gun (a Colt Frontier) and an itch to use it: "And if any moralizing son of a bitch gives me any static, they will fish him out of the river."

Lee fantasizes a brutal imperialism that denies any trace of Cory's compassionate, egalitarian liberalism: note the several references to Napoleon, to ancient Rome, and to German colonialism in Africa and British colonialism in Arabia, as well as the torturer who "did excellent work with the Reds in Barcelona and with the Gestapo in Poland"; Lee's contemptuous mockery of Simón Bolívar, the continent's anticolonial hero, as "The Liberating Fool"; and, of course, the crude muscle of his own "good American dollars." Lee turns the argument inside out and seeks to reverse the demonized position of the queer in cold war America by fully identifying with American power at its most demoniacal. From racially dehumanizing others ("'Taint as if it was being queer," he jokes of sex with Mexican boys, sounding like a Southern redneck) to cracking gags at the expense of the poor (playing up his patrician class identity as one of the "disciplined few") to deriding effeminate homosexuals ("screaming fags") to reviling Jews under cover of respecting them ("The she-Jews—ah, that is, the young Jewish ladies, I must be careful not to lay myself open to a charge of anti-Semitism—done strip teases with Roman intestines"), Lee simultaneously refuses his own status as victim and reveals just how ugly the Ugly American can be.

Queer would not be so unsettling if we could simply call this parody or satire, but it reads more like an act of exorcism—better out than in—of all the voices in Burroughs' head, demons inherited from his class and culture. What makes the odious racism and imperialism of Lee's sick jokes in *Queer* all the more extraordinary is the contrast to *Junky*, where Lee never behaves in this way. In 1953 the Ace Books novel might have passed as a pulp True Confession for most readers, but had *Queer* been published at that time, it is hard to imagine a readership that would not have been sickened. This has less to do with its homosexual theme—it's no more sexually explicit than *Junky*—than with its violent queering of such essential binaries as health and disease, West and East, free world and fascism. *Queer* both conformed to the homophobic logic of the 1950 Senate report—one queer novel like this could pollute the Library of Congress (which, of course, nowadays holds a copy)—*and* earned the same gloss that Burroughs had given Cory's homophile book: enough to turn a man's guts. Little wonder that, like Burroughs himself, *Queer* has continued to remain marginal to gay literary histories and "queer studies."[20]

The hysterical aggression Lee directs outward clearly compensates for the era's feminization of homosexuality as well as for the humiliating frustration in Burroughs' pursuit of Marker. But Lee's fantasy of controlling his lover also betrays Burroughs' fear with respect to the force of his own desire. In Cory's terms, the "invert" struggles "to find a solution to the mystery of his own imperious desires."[21] Lee's fantasies of enslaving others—realized most crudely in his routine of the Slave Trader dealing in boys like used cars—likewise give away his own sense of being a slave to sexual desire. But, surely, the novel still "works" for us today because Lee is a prisoner of love rather than a victim of historically contingent homophobia. Or to put it another way, you don't have to be queer, or to have lived through the 1950s, to recognize *Queer* as an exceptionally dark and compelling anatomy of human (or at least male) desire. Paradoxically, the reason why *Queer* has such a corrosive political as well as emotional power is that Burroughs wrote it out of desire, for a single reader, to a personal audience of one—bluntly stating in October 1952: "I wrote *Queer* for Marker." The queerness of *Queer*, in short, lies not in the facts behind the fiction but in the writing behind the written.

"Some Habits Take Your Gut Along on the Way Out"

When Burroughs began his second novel, he knew the central subject was his relationship with Lewis Marker. On the evidence of *Queer*, that relationship had ended a disastrous failure. But Burroughs did not begin his novel looking backward—far from it. "The boy I went to Ecuador with," he told Ginsberg in November 1951, "is still around and may return there with me. I like him better on closer acquaintance." Although Marker returned to his hometown of Jacksonville, Florida, in January 1952, this was still the situation in March, when Burroughs told Ginsberg he was dedicating *Queer* to "A.L.M. (Adelbert Lewis Marker)" and repeated his plans to return with him to Ecuador.[22] The writing of Burroughs' second novel was not just "about" a past relationship but part of one that still seemed to him full of promise in the present. It was in this sense that he had not decided how to end his novel: "Perhaps the ending just hasn't occurred yet." However, by the time Kerouac arrived in Mexico at the start of May, the situation had taken a dramatic turn. "Marker wrote he isn't coming with me to S.A.," Burroughs reported to Ginsberg on April 22. "I am deeply hurt and disappointed. I will try to change his mind but I don't know." Burroughs tried to change Marker's mind by writing—writing him letters, week after week, despite the absence of replies. "I have written five or six letters to him," Burroughs revealed to Ginsberg in early June, "with fantasies and routines in my best vein but he doesn't answer."

Were these "fantasies and routines" the ones that Lee tells Allerton in *Queer*? Since none of Burroughs' letters to Marker have survived, it's impossible to be sure. However, while *Queer* was well advanced in longhand by the time Burroughs heard that Marker had abandoned him, he almost certainly wrote the Slave Trader routine during that third week of April, and as a sustained fantasy of sexual desire, it is hard to imagine that Burroughs would not have sent it to the very person he desired and so desperately wanted to impress. Or to put it the other way around, the routine that Lee speaks in *Queer* was performed for Marker in writing. Marker's failure to reply to Burroughs' letters throughout April, May, and June surely contributed to the increasingly episodic fragmentation of *Queer*'s narrative, as well as to the ever-more-coercive tone of Lee's routines. When, at the end of May, Ginsberg accused Burroughs of acting like Melville's Captain Ahab, in mad pursuit of his white whale, and of attempting "black magic," Burroughs made no attempt to deny it: "Of course I am attempting black magic. Black magic is always an attempt to force human love, resorted to when there is no other way to score."

If Burroughs now depended on his letter writing to win back Marker, it cannot be a coincidence that the letter in which he reported the traumatic news of Marker's desertion (April 22, 1952) also signals a dramatic departure in his writing. Quite suddenly, and for the first time, it breaks into the wildly extravagant comic-grotesque style of the routine. This was surely one reason Burroughs now asked Ginsberg to save his letters, for they were not just a writer's letters but a crucial part of his writing. Through his letters, the routine gave voice to Burroughs' fantasies, and when reflecting on the form in 1955, he would define it in terms of the epistolary, since "the audience is an integral part of the routine."[23] Generating ever-more-outrageous anecdotes to captivate his reader, the urgency of unreturned desire also laid bare the very drive to control—with all its psychological and political dimensions. This again confirms *Queer* as the secret source for the writing of *Naked Lunch*, whose routines Burroughs would likewise mail out of desire and dependency to an absent lover—Allen Ginsberg. This is not at all the same as saying that Burroughs sent parts of his work in progress to his friends—which any number of authors do—but rather that his trademark form and virtuoso style were driven by his desire-fueled letters and that this practice of writing both drew upon and generated specific kinds of highly performative material. This shared genesis is confirmed by the reappearance in *Naked Lunch* of particular characters from *Queer*—including the "great showman" Tetrazzini and Dry Hole Dutton from the Oil Man routine[24]—and especially by the repeat of the gutting that occurs in the Duc de Ventre's Hispano-Suiza, which makes "a horrible slupping sound." This "slup"[25] is the sound of the routine form itself as a fantasy of devouring desire, emerging like a kind of monstrously extended Freudian "slip." *Queer* may seem mild compared to the toxic feast of *Naked Lunch*, but the violence, and the imagery, run directly from one to the other—as per the poem Burroughs wrote for Marker while he worked on the novel's final sections in June 1952: "The gut unknots and turns over. / 'I'm hungry' / Some habits take your gut along on the way out / Like a mushroom bullet."

That last image also inevitably calls to mind the gunshot that killed Joan Vollmer, and it is impossible to rule out the impact of her death on the writing of *Queer*. Indeed, Lee's tall tales and pathetic acts of macho bravura—which include shooting the head off a mouse ("If you'd got any closer, the mouse would have clogged the muzzle")—

humiliatingly depict a man who is all talk and no trousers, and so recall the situation that fateful night in September 1951 when Joan reportedly goaded her husband by publicly mocking his marksmanship. The self-loathing in Burroughs' self-portrait is haunted by the memory of death as well as the masochism of desire. "Misses Joan terribly," Kerouac observed in May 1952, "lives on in him like mad, vibrating."[26] But the point remains that the specific content and function of Lee's routines in *Queer* can't be accounted for by the shooting of Joan any more than by the effects of drug withdrawal. And having begged the questions in the first place, Burroughs' own partial answers to why he wrote *Queer* should prompt us to piece together the history of his manuscript, to see what happened between its inception in March 1952 and its publication in November 1985.

"I Haven't Discovered the Secret"

The writing of *Queer* is simple enough in outline.[27] Having only started his new novel in mid-March, by April 26 Burroughs had a typed manuscript of twenty-five pages, with seventy more in longhand notes, and on May 14 he mailed Ginsberg a fifty-nine-page typescript. Aware that there were "weak spots,"[28] he immediately made some minor revisions and one week later promised to send "a retyped complete revision of the 60 pages, which supersedes the MS. you now have," which, after a lull in early June, he did on the fifteenth of that month. Burroughs then started "the S.A. sections of *Queer*" and had completed a twenty-five-page typescript by the first week of July. However, the circumstances of neither Burroughs nor his manuscript were so simple.

To begin with, for almost all this time Kerouac was staying with Burroughs—and driving him to distraction by smoking grass in the apartment and never paying his way. Burroughs, meanwhile, was readdicted to heroin and still had to report every Monday at 8:00 a.m. to Lecumberri prison, while waiting for the interminable legal process surrounding Joan's death to take its course. From late April onward, he was also consumed by Marker's desertion. As for his new novel, Burroughs was working under the gun to satisfy the demands of A. A. Wyn at Ace Books, who held up the deal on *Junky* and pressured Burroughs to see a manuscript of the second novel, with thoughts of publishing it added onto the first. Burroughs' manuscript of May 14 was headed "JUNK OR QUEER" in Kerouac's hand, in keeping with Kerouac's conviction that the "title must have indications of both" to double the book's appeal.[29] But Burroughs worked on *Queer* not knowing if Ace would publish it joined to *Junky*, separately, or at all; and when he paused in early June, it was because he was "waiting to hear what Wyn wants." Burroughs wasn't even sure Wyn would let him finish it as a third-person narrative: "Why the Hell can't you shift person in the middle of a book?" he had protested to Ginsberg on April 26. "So it hasn't been done, well let's do it. Anyway I am going to present it third person. If they want to change it, all right, but I think the change would entail considerable loss." The "question of person is confusion's masterpiece,"

Burroughs complained, and when he experimented with making changes, the result was indeed a minor masterpiece of confusion: "I stayed away from the Ship Ahoy for several days," begins one manuscript fragment, "to give Allerton time to forget the bad impression he [*sic*] had undoubtedly made."[30]

The novel's fate was decided in mid-June, when Ginsberg reported, "Wyn don't dig *Queer*."[31] Believing it was still saleable, however, Ginsberg encouraged Burroughs to carry on writing, and on July 6 Burroughs mailed him his South American chapters, after which he did no further work on *Queer*. The manuscript therefore ended at the point of Lee's inconclusive encounter with Dr. Cotter in the jungles outside Puyo, having failed to find the mystery drug *yagé* and with no resolution to his relationship with Allerton. Under different circumstances, Burroughs might possibly have written more—if only to meet Ace's requests, as he did with *Junky*—but it would be a mistake to say he left *Queer* incomplete in the conventional sense.

The fact that his second novel—really a novella—is significantly shorter than *Junky* (itself not a long book) already points toward the even shorter "In Search of Yage" of the following year, this steady reduction in scale emphasizing Burroughs' increasing difficulty in sustaining a continuous, conventionally structured narrative.[32] What would be a crisis for most novelists, however, would prove the making of Burroughs as an experimental writer. In the meantime, it's surely significant that while working on *Queer* and developing his routines, Burroughs also tried his hand at short stories, writing three, later revised and titled "The

Finger," "Driving Lesson," and "Dream of the Penal Colony." Each autobiographical story is tied to *Queer* by precise phrasings and by common narratives of self-destructive desire ending in frustration and failure. The scenario in "Penal Colony" is especially revealing: when the boy that Lee has been trying to seduce breaks off relations, Lee is left in despair because "*I haven't discovered the Secret.*"[33] To some degree, the many references to secrecy in *Queer*— to Russian agents and counterintelligence espionage in Germany, British spies in the Middle East, the cold war search for "thought control" and "confession" drugs—are an extension of this personal drama, and the same goes for the novel's final scene with Dr. Cotter, which emphasizes the hopelessness of Lee's own quest for *yagé*: Cotter "had access to *brujo* secrets. Lee had no such access." In other words, that scene may not be quite as arbitrary and abrupt an ending as it looks. It also finds an echo in Burroughs' resonant conclusion to the prologue of *Junky*: "There is no key, no secret someone else has that he can give you." The context implied that this is the harsh lesson of "the junk equation," but it really summed up the emotional truth of Lee's story of queer desire.

Burroughs wrote the prologue to *Junky* in August 1952, having started on July 6 (the same day he sent Ginsberg the final twenty-five pages of *Queer*) to work on both that introduction and a further forty pages demanded by A. A. Wyn, who had finally sent him a publishing contract. In mid-June Ginsberg had proposed assembling the additional manuscript himself ("They want something covering Mexico, queerness underplayed. . . . I will use *Junk* parts of *Queer* plus letters to fabricate that"),[34] but Burroughs did the work, and at the center of the thirty-eight-page manuscript he mailed to meet a deadline of August 15 were twenty pages culled from the first two chapters of *Queer* (as originally organized), lightly edited and transposed from third to first person. This comprised the opening two and one-half and the last ten pages of chapter 1, plus the last two and one-half pages of chapter 2. He also removed two pages from chapter 3 (the Chimu Bar scene) and two later passages (one about peyote, the other about *yagé*).[35] Altogether, he removed over six thousand words, more than one-third of the May 14 manuscript and about one-fifth of the whole, to make *Junky* up to the length required by Ace Books. In short, no sooner had Burroughs finished writing his second novel than the economic imperatives of publishing made him effectively abandon it by gutting the manuscript to complete his first. The cuts he made during that summer of 1952 would have a profound effect on the book published in 1985. But what happened in the intervening three decades?

At the end of August 1953, Burroughs arrived in New York after his seven-month quest for *yagé* in the jungles of South America and a few weeks' stopover in Mexico City. In Ginsberg's Lower East Side apartment, Burroughs and Ginsberg worked together on the manuscripts of *Queer* and "In Search of Yage,"[36] and during November Alene Lee (fictionalized as Mardou Fox in Kerouac's novel *The Subterraneans*) typed clean copies of both on paper watermarked "Featherweight Onion Skin." Curiously, despite the publication that summer of Ace Books' *Junkie:*

Confessions of an Unredeemed Drug Addict (under the pseudonym William Lee), Burroughs seemed to have decided
that *Queer* was still a viable proposition. Indeed, for the
next four years copies of the manuscript would be circu-
lated by Ginsberg—to the likes of Kenneth Rexroth and
Malcolm Cowley—as the middle part of a three-volume
trilogy, which traveled under the title *Naked Lunch*. In early
1958, Olympia Press—which the following year would
publish the book we now know as *Naked Lunch*—showed
an interest in *Queer* and "Yage," but nothing came of it. By
the time *Naked Lunch* appeared, however, Burroughs' position had decisively changed: "Yage letters by all means," he
wrote Ginsberg in October 1959, "but I really *do not* want
Queer published at this time. It is not representative of
what I do now, and no interest except like an artist's poor
art school sketches—and, as such, I protest." For the next
twenty-five years, whenever interviewers asked about *Queer*
Burroughs would repeat the same judgment—that he considered it "a rather amateurish book."[37] As late as February
1984, he insisted he had no desire to see it published: "It's
like digging out one's high school things."[38] So what happened to change his mind?

In 1984 the so-called Vaduz archive—a massive collection of manuscripts that ten years earlier Burroughs had
sold to Roberto Altman, a financier from Liechtenstein, to
raise desperately needed cash—was purchased and brought
to America by the collector Robert H. Jackson (since 2006
it has been housed in the Berg Collection of the New York
Public Library). As the original catalog prepared by Barry
Miles confirmed, the archive contained a nearly complete

manuscript of *Queer*, the only one that seemed to have survived the years. That is to say, up until this point there was no readily available manuscript to publish, even if Burroughs had wanted to. Meanwhile, the summer of 1984 he left his longtime publisher, Richard Seaver, and literary agent, Peter Matson, when Andrew Wylie managed to broker a seven-book deal with Viking-Penguin, worth $200,000. If the writing of *Queer* was a turning point for Burroughs in the 1950s—its desire-driven, letter-based routines pointing the way beyond straight narrative and toward *Naked Lunch*—so too, thirty years later, was the publication of the novel, which anchored a contract that gave Burroughs financial security for life and shaped the rest of his career. As biographer Ted Morgan observes, "One high point of the deal would be Burroughs' early unpublished novel, *Queer*." "I've worked with William for twenty-five years," Seaver reportedly told Wylie, "and I know he doesn't want to publish *Queer*."[39] But Wylie succeeded where Seaver had failed, and giving first-paragraph prominence to the impending publication of *Queer*, the *New York Times* announced the contract on November 23, 1984. By chance, I was out in Lawrence, Kansas, interviewing Burroughs that same day, nervous on my first visit to the legendary author, asking him about *Queer* and receiving the same answers he had always given—that it was a "trip, it's the oldest form of the novel, going back to Petronius," but at that time "the book people wouldn't touch it . . . said I can't publish this . . . I'd be in jail." The conversation moved on. In retrospect it's clear how unaware I was of the novel's long backstory, or what editing its manuscript might involve, and of course I had no sense of the pain—"painful to an extent I find it difficult to read, let alone to write about"—that Burroughs was about to face as he began his introduction and, together with James Grauerholz, his longtime companion and assistant, prepared to work on his long-lost second novel.

"The Baffling Character of the Unknown"

For all the obvious differences, there was a perverse symmetry to Burroughs' situations in 1952 and 1985 when it came to the publication of *Queer*. Whereas once he had depended on Ginsberg as his amateur literary agent and, as an unknown author, was at the mercy of a pulp publisher, Burroughs now dealt with one of New York's top agents and publishing houses but still found his novel decisively shaped by commercial factors. The key decisions were a consequence of the history of the manuscript's editing thirty years before, which meant that the narrative had lost so much to *Junky* that a similar amount of new material was needed to make the book up to a satisfactory length. And so the text was framed by Burroughs' long introduction at one end and by the addition of "Mexico City Return" as an epilogue at the other.

Burroughs' introduction is sufficiently fascinating in its own right to deserve extensive analysis, but two features stand out. First, there is the draft material that didn't make the final cut. This includes more about Allerton and Denton Welch, and their connection. The English writer is seen as "almost a dead ringer for Allerton," and each is described as "a phantom reader and collaborator," the one credited with inspiring the writing of *Queer* and the other, thirty years after, *The Place of Dead Roads*.[40] There's also an intriguing allusion to D. H. Lawrence's *The Plumed Serpent* (1926), and Burroughs' surprise that this "marvellous magical" account of Mexico made no impression on him at the time of writing *Junky* and *Queer*. Second, a good half of the opening section of the introduction as published, describing life in Mexico City, was taken verbatim from Burroughs' letters (three from September to December 1949, three from January to May 1950, one from May 1951), which accounts for some strange anomalies (when he says, "A single man could live well there for two dollars a day," it's because he was writing to Kerouac) and explains why this material reads more like the narrative of *Queer* than a retrospective account. This last point is the most significant, since it turns out that these opening pages were in fact drafted to fabricate a new first chapter for the novel. This was only one of a range of attempts to reconstruct *Queer*: three further chapters were sketched to fill in gaps in the narrative, a further selection of Burroughs' letters (from 1952) was assembled, and a version of the whole was transposed into the first person. Although James Grauerholz was surely right to not pursue these editorial experiments, they accurately reflected the problems posed by the manuscript on which he and Burroughs had to work—its history complicated by shifts in person, the use of letters, and its gutting for *Junky*. In the end, the 1985 edition did include interpolated letter material, some bridging sections, short expansions, and necessary reorganization (detailed in the endnotes here),[41] but the major addition was "Mexico City Return" as a conclusion— a paradoxical but inspired choice.

Despite its unaccountable shift from third person to first, the epilogue seems a natural continuation of *Queer*'s main narrative. And yet it actually derived from an unused manuscript intended to conclude "Yage," and was written in July 1953 during Burroughs' stopover in Mexico City en route to New York.[42] What seems to be a description of Lee returning to Mexico after his trip with Allerton, based on events in late summer 1951, is in fact a description of his return a full two years later. This in turn explains various anomalies, such as Lee's anxiety at Mexico City airport—the result of Burroughs' legal status in Mexico since the shooting of Joan. And yet "Mexico City Return" belongs with *Queer* more than with "In Search of Yage," not only as a conclusion to Burroughs' Mexican-set narrative and for the return of Allerton, but, above all, for its final routine. Here, Lee's dream of the menacing Skip Tracer sums up the lingering nightmare of Burroughs' desire, while his condition of being possessed by both desire and writing is underlined by an aside on the manuscript stating that it came to him, "Like taking dictation." The echo of the routines in *Queer* is no coincidence, and it is entirely fitting that this routine is haunted by phrases from F. Scott Fitzgerald's uncanny tale of love and evil possession "A Short Trip Home," which Burroughs had already used in *Queer* and which gives this denouement its creepy lyricism.[43] Something of this eerie quality is caught by the slow, softly spoken recitative in Erling Wold's superb operatic adaptation of *Queer* (2000), but the closest parallel to the sinister twist Burroughs gives the theme of lovesickness might be Roy Orbison's ballad "In Dreams," as lip-synched by Dean Stockwell to nightmarish effect in David Lynch's film *Blue Velvet*. The Skip Tracer is Burroughs' noir Sandman, a creature of the dream dimension and the perfect finale for *Queer*.[44]

There remains one final surprise regarding the 1985 publication: the manuscript of *Queer* on which it was based is the original, unrevised version Burroughs sent Ginsberg on May 14, 1952. This is clear not only from its length and roughness—it is composed on six different paper types with almost all pages showing hand or typed corrections—but from precise references in contemporaneous letters. In the years since, only one of the three pages missing from this first manuscript has turned up—the ending of the lost "Panama" chapter, found misfiled in the Berg Collection—while further research has located just fragments of the two later *Queer* manuscripts. Although Burroughs told Ginsberg that he had gone over his first draft, "adding, cutting out, altering," the three pages that survive from the second draft (one held at Columbia, two at Stanford University) show only very minor changes.[45] Likewise, the five-page sequence from the start of the third and final draft cleanly typed by Alene Lee in 1953 (and also held by Stanford) reveals only minor revisions. Whether Burroughs and Ginsberg did make major changes in 1953 is unlikely but remains unknown. This new edition of *Queer* is therefore based substantially on the same sources as the 1985 edition, and given the rigor of James Grauerholz's editing then, the most significant differences lie not in the text itself but in its presentation. I have taken the opportunity, which Grauerholz felt was premature twenty-five years ago, to make visible its backstory and to make explicit the editorial process. That said, editing is an act of interpretation, and my own understanding of *Queer* is reflected in those changes that have—and have not—been made for this new edition.

First, I have preserved a little more of the roughness in Burroughs' manuscript, not making a number of very small corrections that, while they had Burroughs' imprimatur, seemed to me to improve the writing more than the necessary minimum. And second, as well as reediting and retitling the epilogue (now, "Two Years Later: Mexico City Return") and re-creating the "Panama" chapter (chapter 7), I have made a number of short insertions of material that was either previously unused or unavailable—roughly five hundred words in the notes and just over a thousand in the text. The bulk of the insertions follow decisions taken regarding the material removed from *Queer* in 1952 for *Junky*. That cannibalization had the signal effect of making *Queer* all the queerer, since what Burroughs removed was everything that truly overlapped, leaving behind what could never have been considered "Part II" of his first novel. Of all the various options for restoring to *Queer* what had been cut for *Junky*, it seemed right to reinstate just one section, Lee's visit to the Chimu Bar, which fits better in Burroughs' second novel. That this material now appears in both *Junky* and *Queer*, though odd, is no more than a logical extension of the striking textual fluidity and extreme contingency that always characterized Burroughs' first trilogy. My aim in reediting all three texts has been to clarify their history and to re-present them with the scholarly care their importance deserves, not to undo the past or claim to straighten everything out. In fact, the key decision in this respect was to resist the temptation to restore the two and one-half pages with which *Queer* originally began. Starting, "One morning in April Lee woke up a little sick," this is an odd passage in *Junky* and a crucial one for interpretations of *Queer*—since it would explain Lee's behavior as the physiological and psychological effects of drug withdrawal—and it's for this reason, rather than despite it, that the material was left out. For the one thing that would make *Queer* untrue to its title would be to explain away all that makes it so mysterious and unsettling a novel in the first place. In 1952 Burroughs reviled Donald Webster Cory's book, but he too might have wondered: "Is it, perhaps, in the baffling character of the unknown that there can be found the origin and significance of the word *queer*?"[46]

Oliver Harris
November 2009

1. Jack Kerouac, *Selected Letters, 1940–1956*, edited by Ann Charters (New York: Viking, 1995), 352.

2. Unless stated otherwise, all quotations from Burroughs' letters are from *The Letters of William S. Burroughs, 1945–1959*, edited by Oliver Harris (New York: Viking, 1993).

3. Officially, the park is named after José de San Martín, the Argentine general whose historic 1822 meeting with Simón Bolívar is commemorated in the monument, La Rotonda, Lee describes in Guayaquil.

4. Jorge García-Robles, *La bala perdida: William S. Burroughs en México (1949–1952)* (Mexico: Ediciones del Milenio, 1995), 91 (my translation).

5. On the title's origins in these lines, see the endnote in this edition (page 140) and my essay "The Beginnings of '*Naked Lunch*, an Endless Novel,'" in *Naked Lunch@50: Anniversary Essays* (Carbondale: Southern Illinois University Press, 2009), 14–25.

6. In early April Burroughs wrote to Kerouac, "I think the title *Queer* for second section is only terrific. The title had me baffled." On the twenty-second of the month, Burroughs clarified his understanding of the term when reacting with outrage to the provocative idea of Carl Solomon, then working for his uncle A. A. Wyn at Ace Books, that the novel be called *Fag*. See Burroughs, *Letters*, 119–21.

7. Examples of the presence of *Queer* in *Doctor Sax* (1959)

include references to Isadora Duncan, Napoleon brandy, and Chimu centipedes; the phrases "whore-caster" and "words sibilantly cracking"; and resemblances between Kerouac's "evil Gidean" and the Slave Trader routine, and between Burroughs/Lee and Sax, who "looked a little bit like Bull Hubbard (tall, thin, plain, strange)."

8. Kerouac, *Letters*, 356.

9. Donald Webster Cory, *The Homosexual in America* (New York: Greenberg, 1951), 167. Cory was a pseudonym for Edward Sagarin.

10. This is, in fact, surprising, not so much because of the biographical points of intersection between Burroughs and Vidal—patrician gay Americans whose educations overlapped (at Los Alamos Ranch School) and who wrote largely as expatriates in Europe—but because of the similarities between their early writing. Like *Queer*, *The City and the Pillar* details a series of gay social scenes and subcultures; like *Queer* it features Mexican locations (Yucatán and Mérida); and Vidal's presentation of sexual obsession aiming for a Platonic reunion, the "discovery of a twin," finds an echo in Lee's even more obsessive and narcissistic fantasies of bodily merger with Allerton.

11. With its Greenwich Village setting and coauthorship, *The Young and Evil* is echoed in the 1945 Burroughs-Kerouac collaboration *And the Hippos Were Boiled in Their Tanks*.

12. Allen Ginsberg, *The Book of Martyrdom and Artifice* (New York: Da Capo, 2006), 78. Burroughs included Jackson in an October 1944 reading list that featured such other gay-themed books as *Maiden Voyage* (1943) by Denton Welch and Richard Brooks' *The Brick Foxhole* (1945), the latter filmed as *Crossfire* (1947) but with the original theme of homophobia replaced by anti-Semitism. Kerouac cites Jackson's novel in *And the Hippos Were Boiled in Their Tanks* (New York: Grove, 2008), 177.

13. Charles Jackson, *The Lost Weekend* (London: Penguin, 1989), 32, 38.

14. Burroughs would surely have been struck by the coincidence that what traumatized Birnam—the discovery of an adolescent love letter: "hero-worship stuff, but pretty passionate" (86)— echoed the diary of homosexual longings he himself had kept at Los Alamos and whose public exposure, he always claimed, put him off writing for years afterward.

15. Cory, 176, 172.

16. Burroughs (1981) in *Burroughs Live: The Collected Interviews of William S. Burroughs 1960–1997*, edited by Sylvère Lotringer (Los Angeles: Semiotext(e), 2001), 520; see also 246, 597.

17. Quoted in John D'Emilio, *Sexual Politics, Sexual Communities* (Chicago: University of Chicago Press, 1983), 37.

18. Cory, 150.

19. Cory, 152.

20. On this topic, see Jamie Russell, *Queer Burroughs* (New York: Palgrave, 2001). On the critical response to *Queer*, see my *William Burroughs and the Secret of Fascination* (Carbondale: Southern Illinois University Press, 2003), 78–132.

21. Cory, 153.

22. Burroughs used the cryptic dedication planned for *Queer* when *Junkie* was published in April 1953—a decision that sheds light on both his relationship with Marker and his expectations regarding the publication of *Queer*. The dedication ("To A.L.M.") was removed from the reedited *Junky* of 1977.

23. William S. Burroughs, *Interzone* (New York: Viking, 1989), 127.

24. The Oil Man routine drew on Burroughs' experience of Texas wildcatters and made use of colorful anecdotes he heard from his friend Kells Elvins, including ones about a

certain David Harold "Dry Hole" Byrd. For this and other important connections between Burroughs' life and *Queer*, see Rob Johnson, *The Lost Years of William S. Burroughs: Beats in South Texas* (College Station: Texas A&M University Press, 2006), 93–99.

25. Burroughs spelled the term in three different ways in his manuscripts: "slup," "shlup," and "schlup." In the Duc de Ventre passage in *Queer*, the spelling is "slup" and "slupping"—restored for this edition, having been amended in 1985 to "shlup"—and in the equivalent passage in *Naked Lunch*, "schlup" and "schlupping." In Burroughs' letter of June 24, 1954, he refers to the way routines "shlup" over into real action. In his letter of April 22, 1952, he gives Ginsberg a "sluppy" kiss, suggesting his spelling was consistent at the time of *Queer*.

26. Kerouac, *Letters*, 353.

27. The one complication is the "Mexican section" Burroughs wrote in the spring of 1951 to add to his "Junk" manuscript and which concerned the "connections between junk and sex"; it's unclear what this comprised or if parts ended up in *Queer* and/or *Junky*.

28. Burroughs to Ginsberg, May 15, 1952 (Ginsberg Collection, Columbia University); line not in the published version.

29. Kerouac, *Letters*, 353.

30. In the Allen Ginsberg Papers, Stanford University, Correspondence 1, Box 2, Folder 42.

31. *The Letters of Allen Ginsberg*, edited by Bill Morgan (New York: Da Capo, 2008), 77.

32. Roughly, the 1950 "Junk" manuscript is 38,000 words and the 1953 edition 47,000; the full *Queer* manuscript is 31,000 words; the fullest "Yage" manuscript is 20,000 words and the first printing of "In Search of Yage" 12,000.

33. Burroughs, *Interzone*, 45.

34. Ginsberg, *Letters*, 77.

35. See *Junky: The Definitive Text of "Junk"* (New York: Penguin, 2003), 105–16, 93–94, 117–19, 122–23, 127.

36. For the manuscript and editing history of "Yage," see my introduction to *The Yage Letters Redux* (San Francisco: City Lights, 2006).

37. Burroughs (1974), in Lotringer, 272.

38. Burroughs (1984), in Lotringer, 597.

39. Ted Morgan, *Literary Outlaw: The Life and Times of William S. Burroughs* (New York: Henry Holt, 1988), 596–99.

40. *Queer* 1985 editorial files, William S. Burroughs Papers, Folio 3, Berg Collection, New York Public Library.

41. The endnotes document the history and use of the manuscripts, rather than note every difference between the two editions. They do detail all significant insertions made for the 1985 edition and any not retained here. From the point of view of the 1985 text, there are, aside from spelling and punctuation changes and a very few outright corrections, about a hundred cases where the original manuscript has been preferred and/or small inserts from 1985 removed.

42. For a detailed account, see my introduction to *Everything Lost: The Latin American Notebook of William S. Burroughs* (Columbus: Ohio State University Press, 2008).

43. Burroughs used "A Short Trip Home" for the description of Winston Moor; see the note on these lines in this edition.

44. Like an unlaid ghost, Allerton returns throughout the Burroughs oeuvre, from his appearance as a "phantom" in *The Soft Machine* (Paris: Olympia, 1961), 173, to two dreams in *My Education* (New York: Viking, 1995), 93, 114.

45. See the "Key to Manuscripts" in the endnotes.

46. Cory, 22.

CHAPTER 1

Lee turned his attention to a Jewish boy named Carl Steinberg he had known casually for about a year. The first time he saw Carl, Lee thought, "I could use that, if the family jewels weren't in pawn to Uncle Junk."

The boy was blond, his face thin and sharp with a few freckles, always a little pink around the ears and nose like he had just washed. Lee had never known anyone to look as clean as Carl. With his small round brown eyes and fuzzy blond hair, he reminded Lee of a young bird. Born in Munich, Carl had grown up in Baltimore. In manner and outlook he seemed European. He shook hands with traces of a heel click. In general, Lee found European youths easier to talk to than Americans. The rudeness of many Americans depressed him, a rudeness based on a solid ignorance of the whole concept of manners and on the proposition that for social purposes all people are more or less equal and interchangeable.

What Lee looked for in any relationship was the feel of contact. He felt some contact with Carl. The boy listened politely and seemed to understand what Lee was saying. After some initial balking, he accepted the fact of Lee's sexual interest in his person. He told Lee, "Since I can't change my mind about you, I will have to change my mind about other things."

But Lee soon found out he could make no progress. "If I got this far with an American kid," he reasoned, "I could get the rest of the way. So he's not queer. People can be obliging. What is the obstacle?" Lee finally guessed the answer: "What makes it impossible is that his mother wouldn't like it." Lee knew it was time to pack in. He recalled a homosexual Jewish friend who lived in Oklahoma City. Lee had asked, "Why do you live here? You have enough money to live anywhere you like." The reply was, "It would kill my mother if I moved away." Lee had been speechless.

One afternoon Lee was walking with Carl by the Amsterdam Avenue park. Suddenly Carl bowed slightly and shook Lee's hand. "Best of luck," he said, and ran for a streetcar.

Lee stood looking after him, then walked over into the park and sat down on a concrete bench that was molded to resemble wood. Blue flowers from a blossoming tree had fallen on the bench and on the walk in front of it. Lee sat there watching the flowers move along the path in a warm spring wind. The sky was clouding up for an afternoon shower. Lee felt lonely and defeated. "I'll have to look for someone else," he thought. He covered his face with his hands. He was very tired.

He saw a shadowy line of boys. As each boy came to the front of the line, he said, "Best of luck," and ran for a streetcar.

"Sorry . . . wrong number . . . try again . . . somewhere else . . . someplace else . . . not here . . . not me . . . can't use it, don't need it, don't want it . . . sorry. . . . Why pick on me?" The last face was so real and so ugly, Lee said aloud, "Who asked you, you ugly son of a bitch?"

Lee opened his eyes and looked around. Two Mexican adolescents walked by, their arms around each other's necks. He looked after them, licking his dry, cracked lips.

Lee continued to see Carl after that, until finally Carl said, "Best of luck" for the last time, and walked away. Lee heard later he had gone with his family to Uruguay.

Lee was sitting with Winston Moor in the Rathskeller, drinking double tequilas. Cuckoo clocks and moth-eaten deer heads gave the Rathskeller a dreary, out-of-place, Tyrolean look. A smell of spilt beer, overflowing toilets, and sour garbage hung in the place like a thick fog and drifted out into the street through narrow, inconvenient swinging doors. A television set was out of order half the time and emitted horrible, guttural squawks like a Frankenstein monster.

"I was in here last night," Lee said to Moor. "Got talking to a queer doctor and his boyfriend. The doc is a major in the Medical Corps, the boyfriend some kind of vague engineer. Awful-looking little bitch. So the doctor invites me to have a drink with them, and the boyfriend is getting jealous, and I don't want a beer anyway, which the doctor takes as a reflection on Mexico and on his own person. He begins the do-you-like-Mexico routine. So I tell him Mexico is O.K., some of it, but he personally is a pain in the ass. Told him this in a nice way, you understand. Besides, I had to go home to my wife in any case.

"So he says, 'You don't have any wife, you are just as queer as I am.' I told him, 'I don't know how queer you are, Doc, and I ain't about to find out. It isn't as if you was a good-looking Mexican. You're a goddamned old, ugly-looking Mexican. And that goes double for your moth-eaten boyfriend.' I was hoping, of course, the deal wouldn't come to any extreme climax. . . .

"You never knew Hatfield? Of course not. Before your time. He killed a *cargador* in a *pulquería*. The deal cost him five hundred dollars. Now, figuring a *cargador* as rock bottom, think how much it would cost you to shoot a major in the Mexican Army."

Moor called the waiter over. "*Yo quiero un sandwich,*" he said, smiling at the waiter. "*¿Quel sandwiches tiene?*"

"What do you want?" Lee asked, annoyed at the interruption.

"I don't know exactly," said Moor, looking through the menu. "I wonder if they could make me a melted cheese sandwich on toasted whole-wheat bread." Moor turned back to the waiter, with a smile that was supposed to be boyish.

Lee closed his eyes as Moor launched an attempt to

convey the concept of melted cheese on whole-wheat toast. Moor was being charmingly helpless with his inadequate Spanish. He was putting down a little-boy-in-a-foreign-country routine. Moor smiled into an inner mirror, a smile without a trace of warmth, but it was not a cold smile: it was the meaningless smile of senile decay, the smile that goes with false teeth, the smile of a man grown old and stir-simple in the solitary confinement of exclusive self-love.

Moor was a thin young man with blond hair that was habitually somewhat long. He had pale blue eyes and very white skin. There were dark patches under his eyes and two deep lines around the mouth. He looked like a child, and at the same time like a prematurely aged man. His face showed the ravages of the death process, the inroads of decay in flesh cut off from the living charge of contact. Moor was motivated, literally kept alive and moving, by hate, but there was no passion or violence in his hate. Moor's hate was a slow, steady push, weak but infinitely persistent, waiting to take advantage of any weakness in another. The slow drip of Moor's hate had etched the lines of decay in his face. He had aged without experience of life, like a piece of meat rotting on a pantry shelf.

Moor made a practice of interrupting a story just before the point was reached. Often he would start a long conversation with a waiter or anybody else handy, or he would go vague and distant, yawn, and say, "What was that?" as though recalled to dull reality from reflections of which others could have no concept.

Moor began talking about his wife, Jackie. "At first, Bill, she was so dependent on me that she used literally to have hysterics when I had to go to the museum where I work. I managed to build up her ego to the point where she didn't need me, and after that the only thing I could do was leave. There was nothing more I could do for her."

Moor was putting down his sincere act. "My God," Lee thought, "he really believes it."

Lee ordered another double tequila. Moor stood up. "Well, I have to be going," he said. "I have a lot of things to do."

"Well, listen," said Lee. "How about dinner tonight?"

Moor said, "Well, all right."

"At six in the K.C. Steak House."

"All right." Moor left.

Lee drank half the tequila the waiter put in front of him. He had known Moor off and on in N.Y. for several years and never liked him. Moor disliked Lee, but then Moor didn't like anybody. Lee said to himself, "You must be crazy, making passes in that direction, when you know what a bitch he is. These borderline characters can out-bitch any fag."

When Lee arrived at the K.C. Steak House, Moor was already there, and with him he had Tom Williams, another Salt Lake City boy. Lee thought, "He brought along a chaperone."

"I like the guy, Tom, but I can't stand to be alone with him. He keeps trying to go to bed with me. That's what I don't like about queers. You can't keep it on a basis of friendship. . . ." Yes, Lee could hear that conversation.

During dinner Moor and Williams talked about a boat

they planned to build at Zihuatanejo. Lee thought this was a silly project. "Boat building is a job for a professional, isn't it?" Lee asked. Moor pretended not to hear.

After dinner Lee walked back to Moor's rooming house with Moor and Williams. At the door Lee asked, "Would you gentlemen care for a drink? I'll get a bottle. . . ." He looked from one to the other.

Moor said, "Well, no. You see, we want to work on the plans for this boat we are going to build."

"Oh," said Lee. "Well, I'll see you tomorrow. How about meeting me for a drink in the Rathskeller? Say around five."

"Well, I expect I'll be busy tomorrow."

"Yes, but you have to eat and drink."

"Well, you see, this boat is more important to me than anything right now. It will take up all my time."

Lee said, "Suit yourself," and walked away.

Lee was deeply hurt. He could hear Moor saying, "Thanks for running interference, Tom. Well, I hope he got the idea. Of course Lee is an interesting guy and all that . . . but this queer situation is just more than I can take." Tolerant, looking at both sides of the question, sympathetic up to a point, finally forced to draw a tactful but firm line. "And he really believes that," Lee thought. "Like that crap about building up his wife's ego. He can revel in the satisfactions of virulent bitchiness and simultaneously see himself as a saint. Quite a trick."

Actually, Moor's brush-off was calculated to inflict the maximum hurt possible under the circumstances. It put Lee in the position of a detestably insistent queer, too stupid and too insensitive to realize that his attentions were not wanted, forcing Moor to the distasteful necessity of drawing a diagram.

Lee leaned against a lamppost for several minutes. The shock had sobered him, drained away his drunken euphoria. He realized how tired he was, and how weak, but he was not ready yet to go home.

CHAPTER 2

"**E**verything made in this country falls apart," Lee thought. He was examining the blade of his stainless-steel pocketknife. The chrome plating was peeling off like silver paper. "Wouldn't surprise me if I picked up a boy in the Alameda and his . . . Here comes Honest Joe."

Joe Guidry sat down at the table with Lee, dropping bundles on the table and in the empty chair. He wiped off the top of a beer bottle with his sleeve and drank half the beer in a long gulp. He was a large man with a politician's red Irish face.

"What you know?" Lee asked.

"Not much, Lee. Except someone stole my typewriter. And I know who took it. It was that Brazilian, or whatever he is. You know him. Maurice."

"Maurice? Is that the one you had last week? The wrestler?"

"You mean Louie, the gym instructor. No, this is another one. Louie has decided all that sort of thing is very wrong, and he tells me that I am going to burn in hell but *he* is going to heaven."

"Serious?"

"Oh, yes. Well, Maurice is as queer as I am." Joe belched. "Excuse me. If not queerer. But he won't accept it. I think stealing my typewriter is a way he takes to demonstrate to me and to himself that he is just in it for all he can get. As a matter of fact, he's so queer I've lost interest in him. Not completely though. When I see the little bastard, I'll most likely invite him back to my apartment instead of beating the shit out of him like I should."

Lee tipped his chair back against the wall and looked around the room. Someone was writing a letter at the next table. If he had overheard the conversation, he gave no sign. The proprietor was reading the bullfight section of the paper, spread out on the counter in front of him. A silence peculiar to Mexico seeped into the room, a vibrating, soundless hum.

Joe finished his beer, wiped his mouth with the back of his hand, and stared at the wall with watery, bloodshot blue eyes. The silence seeped into Lee's body, and his face went slack and blank. The effect was curiously spectral, as though you could see through his face. The face was ravaged and vicious and old, but the clear green eyes were dreamy and innocent. His light brown hair was extremely fine and would not stay combed. Generally it fell down across his forehead, and on occasion brushed the food he was eating or got in his drink.

"Well, I have to be going," said Joe. He gathered up his bundles and nodded to Lee, bestowing on him one of his sweet politician smiles, and walked out, his fuzzy, half-bald head outlined for a moment in the sunlight before he disappeared from Lee's view.

Lee yawned and picked up a comic section from the next table. It was two days old. He put it down and yawned again. He got up and paid for his drink and walked out into the late afternoon sun. He had no place to go, so he went over to Sears' magazine counter and read the new magazines for free.

He cut back past the K.C. Steak House. Moor beckoned to him from inside the restaurant. Lee went in and sat down at a table with Moor. "You look terrible," he said. He knew that was what Moor wanted to hear. As a matter of fact, Moor did look worse than usual. He had always been pale; now he was yellowish.

The boat project had fallen through. Moor and Williams and Williams' wife, Lil, were back from Zihuatanejo. Moor was not on speaking terms with the Williamses.

Lee ordered a pot of tea. Moor started talking about Lil. "You know, Lil ate the cheese down there. She ate everything and she never got sick. She won't go to a doctor. One morning she woke up blind in one eye and she could barely see out the other. But she wouldn't have a doctor. In a few days she could see again, good as ever. I was hoping she'd go blind."

Lee realized Moor was perfectly serious. "He's insane," Lee thought.

Moor went on about Lil. She had made advances to him, of course. He had paid more than his share of the rent and food. She was a terrible cook. They had left him there sick. He shifted to the subject of his health. "Just let me show you my urine test," Moor said with boyish enthusiasm. He spread the piece of paper out on the table. Lee looked at it without interest.

"Look here." Moor pointed. "Urea thirteen. Normal is fifteen to twenty-two. Is that serious, do you think?"

"I'm sure I don't know."

"And traces of sugar. What does the whole picture mean?" Moor obviously considered the question of intense interest.

"Why don't you take it to a doctor?"

"I did. He said he would have to take a twenty-four-hour test, that is, samples of urine over a twenty-four-hour period, before he could express any opinion. . . . You know, I have a dull pain in the chest, right here. I wonder if it could be tuberculosis?"

"Take an X-ray."

"I did. The doctor is going to take a skin reaction test. Oh, another thing, I think I have undulant fever. Do you think I have fever now?" He pushed his forehead forward for Lee to feel. Lee felt an earlobe. "I don't think so," he said.

Moor went on and on, following the circular route of the true hypochondriac, back to tuberculosis and the urine test. Lee thought he had never heard anything as tiresome and depressing. Moor did not have tuberculosis or kidney trouble or undulant fever. He was sick with the sickness of death. Death was in every cell of his body. He gave off a faint, greenish steam of decay. Lee imagined he would glow in the dark.

Moor talked with boyish eagerness. "I think I need an operation."

Lee said he really had to go.

Lee turned down Coahuila. He walked with one foot falling directly in front of the other, always fast and purposeful, as if he were leaving the scene of a holdup. He passed a group in expatriate uniform: red-checked shirts outside the belt, blue jeans, and beards, and another group of young men in conventional, if shabby, clothes. Among these Lee recognized a boy named Eugene Allerton. Allerton was tall and very thin, with high cheekbones, a small bright-red mouth, and amber-colored eyes that took on a faint violet flush when he was drunk. His gold-brown hair was differentially bleached by the sun like a sloppy dyeing job. He had straight black eyebrows and black eyelashes. An equivocal face, very young, clean-cut, and boyish, at the same time conveying an impression of makeup, delicate and exotic and Oriental. Allerton was never completely neat or clean, but you did not think of him as being dirty. He was simply careless and lazy to the point of appearing, at times, only half-awake. Often he did not hear what someone said a foot from his ear. "Pellagra, I expect," thought Lee sourly. He nodded to Allerton and smiled. Allerton nodded, as if surprised, and did not smile.

Lee walked on, a little depressed. "Perhaps I can accomplish something in that direction. . . . Well, *a ver.* . . ." He froze in front of a restaurant like a bird dog: "Hungry. . . . Quicker to eat here than buy something and cook it." When Lee was hungry, when he wanted a drink or a shot of morphine, delay was unbearable.

He went in, ordered steak *a la Mexicana* and a glass of milk, and waited with his mouth watering for food. A young man with a round face and a loose mouth came into the restaurant. Lee said, "Hello, Horace," in a clear voice. Horace nodded without speaking and sat down as far from Lee as he could get in the small restaurant. Lee smiled. His food arrived and he ate quickly, like an animal, cramming bread and steak into his mouth and washing it down with gulps of milk. He leaned back in his chair and lit a cigarette.

"*Un café solo,*" he called to the waitress as she walked by, carrying a pineapple soda to two young Mexicans in double-breasted pinstripe suits. One of the Mexicans had moist brown pop eyes and a scraggly moustache of greasy black hairs. He looked pointedly at Lee, and Lee looked away. "Careful," he thought, "or he will be over here asking me how I like Mexico." He dropped his half-smoked cigarette into half an inch of cold coffee, walked over to the counter, paid the bill, and was out of the restaurant before the Mexican could formulate an opening sentence. When Lee decided to leave someplace, his departure was abrupt.

The Ship Ahoy had a few phony hurricane lamps by way of a nautical atmosphere. Two small rooms with tables, the bar in one room, and four high, precarious stools. The place was always dimly lit and sinister looking. The patrons were tolerant but in no way bohemian. The bearded set never frequented the Ship Ahoy. The place existed on borrowed time, without a liquor license, under many changes of management. At this time it was run by an American named Tom Weston and an American-born Mexican.

Lee walked directly to the bar and ordered a drink. He drank it and ordered a second before looking around the room to see if Allerton was there. Allerton was alone at a table, tipped back in a chair with one leg crossed over the other, holding a bottle of beer on his knee. He nodded to Lee. Lee tried to achieve a greeting at once friendly and casual, designed to show interest without pushing a short acquaintance. The result was ghastly.

As Lee stood aside to bow in his dignified old-world greeting, there emerged instead a leer of naked lust, wrenched in the pain and hate of his deprived body and, in simultaneous double exposure, a sweet child's smile of liking and trust, shockingly out of time and place, mutilated and hopeless.

Allerton was appalled. "Perhaps he has some sort of a tic," he thought. He decided to remove himself from contact with Lee before the man did something even more distasteful. The effect was like a cut connection. Allerton was not cold or hostile; Lee simply wasn't there so far as he was concerned. Lee looked at him helplessly for a moment, then turned back to the bar, defeated and shaken.

Lee finished his second drink. When he looked around again, Allerton was playing chess with Mary, an American girl with dyed red hair and carefully applied makeup, who had come into the bar in the meantime. "Why waste time here?" Lee thought. He paid for the two drinks and walked out.

The Chimu Bar looks like any cantina from the outside, but as soon as you walk in you know you are in a queer bar.

Lee ordered a drink at the bar and looked around. Three Mexican fags were posturing in front of the jukebox. One of them slithered over to where Lee was standing, with the stylized gestures of a temple dancer, and asked for a cigarette. Lee watched them from an inner silence. He registered something archaic in the stylized movements, a depraved animal grace at once beautiful and repulsive. He could see them moving in the light of campfires, the ambiguous gestures shadowed out into the dark. Sodomy is as old as the human species.

One of the fags was sitting in a booth by the jukebox, perfectly immobile with a stupid animal serenity.

Lee turned to get a closer look at the boy on his right. "Not bad," he thought. "*¿Por qué si triste?*" he asked. Not much of a gambit, but he wasn't there to converse.

The boy smiled, revealing very red gums and sharp

teeth far apart. He shrugged and said something to the effect that he wasn't *triste* or not especially so. Lee looked around the room.

"*Vámonos a otro lugar,*" he said.

The boy nodded. They walked down the street into an all-night restaurant and sat down in a booth. The boy dropped a hand onto Lee's leg under the table. Lee felt his stomach knot with excitement. He gulped his coffee and waited impatiently while the boy finished a beer and smoked a cigarette.

The boy knew a hotel. Lee pushed five pesos through a grill. An old man unlocked the door of a room and dropped a ragged towel on the chair. "*¿Llevas pistola?*" asked the boy. He had caught sight of Lee's pistol. Lee placed the weapon on safe. "Yes, I carry a pistol."

He folded his pants and dropped them over a chair, placing the pistol on his pants. He dropped his shirt and shorts on the pistol. Though he was near forty, Lee had the thin body of an adolescent. His shoulders and chest were wide across and very shallow. The line of his body curved in from the chest to a flat stomach. Body hair was sparse and dark in contrast to the light brown hair of his head.

Lee sat down naked on the edge of the bed and watched the boy finish undressing. The boy was folding his worn blue suit with care. He took off his shirt and placed it around his coat on the back of a chair. His skin was smooth and copper colored. The boy stepped out of his shorts and turned around and smiled at Lee. Then he came and sat beside him on the bed. Lee ran one hand slowly over the boy's back, following with the other hand the curve of the chest down over the flat brown stomach. The boy smiled and lay down on the bed. Lee's body was moving in rhythmic contractions, every muscle caressing the smooth hard body of the other, the amoeba reflex to surround and incorporate. His body tensed convulsively rigid, sparks flashed behind his eyes and the breath whistled through his teeth. Slowly his muscles relaxed away from the other's body.

They both smoked a cigarette, their shoulders touching under the covers. The boy said he had to go. They both dressed. Lee wondered if the boy expected money. He decided not. Outside, they separated at a corner, shaking hands.

At that time the G.I. students patronized Lola's during the daytime and the Ship Ahoy at night. Lola's was not exactly a bar. It was a small beer-and-soda joint. There was a Coca-Cola box full of beer and soda and ice at the left of the door as you came in. A counter with tube-metal stools covered in yellow glazed leather ran down one side of the room as far as the jukebox. Tables were lined along the wall opposite the counter. The stools had long since lost the rubber caps for the legs and made horrible screeching noises when the maid pushed them around to sweep. There was a kitchen in back, where a slovenly cook fried everything in rancid fat. There was neither past nor future in Lola's. The place was a waiting room, where certain people checked in at certain times.

Several days after his pickup in the Chimu, Lee was sitting in Lola's, reading aloud from *Últimas Notícias* to Jim Cochan. There was a story about a man who murdered his wife and children. Cochan looked about for a means to escape, but every time he made a move to go, Lee pinned him down with: "Get a load of this. . . . 'When his wife came home from the market, her husband, already drunk, was brandishing his .45.' Why do they always have to brandish it?"

Lee read to himself for a moment. Cochan stirred uneasily. "Jesus Christ," said Lee, looking up. "After he killed his wife and three children he takes a razor and puts on a suicide act." He returned to the paper: "'But resulted only with scratches that did not require medical attention.' What a slobbish performance!" He turned the page and began reading the leads half-aloud: "They're cutting the butter with Vaseline. Fine thing. Lobster with drawn K-Y. . . . Here's a man was surprised in his taco stand with a dressed-down dog . . . a great long skinny hound dog at that. There's a picture of him posing in front of his taco stand with the dog. . . . One citizen asked another for a light. The party in second part don't have a match so first part pulls an ice pick and kills him. Murder is the national neurosis of Mexico."

Cochan stood up. Lee was on his feet instantly. "Sit down on your ass, or what's left of it after four years in the navy," he said.

"I got to go."

"What are you, henpecked?"

"No kidding. I been out too much lately. My old lady . . ."

Lee wasn't listening. He had just seen Allerton stroll by outside the door and look in. Allerton had not greeted him but walked on after a momentary pause. "I was in the shadow," Lee thought. "He couldn't see me from the door." He did not notice Cochan's departure.

On a sudden impulse he rushed out the door. Allerton was half a block away. Lee overtook him. Allerton turned, raising his eyebrows, which were straight and black as a pen stroke. He looked surprised and a bit alarmed, since he was dubious of Lee's sanity. Lee improvised desperately.

"I just wanted to tell you Mary was in Lola's a little while ago. She asked me to tell you she would be in the Ship Ahoy later on, around five." This was partly true. Mary had been in and had asked Lee if he had seen Allerton.

Allerton was relieved. "Oh, thank you," he said, quite cordial now. "Will you be around tonight?"

"Yes, I think so." Lee nodded and smiled, and turned away quickly.

Lee left his apartment for the Ship Ahoy just before five. Allerton was sitting at the bar. Lee sat down and ordered a drink, then turned to Allerton with a casual greeting, as though they were on familiar and friendly terms. Allerton returned the greeting automatically before he realized that Lee had somehow established himself on a familiar basis, whereas he had previously decided to have as little to do with Lee as possible. Allerton had a talent for ignoring people, but he was not competent at dislodging someone from a position already occupied.

Lee began talking—casual, unpretentiously intelligent,

dryly humorous. Slowly he dispelled Allerton's impression that he was a peculiar and undesirable character. When Mary arrived, Lee greeted her with a tipsy old-world gallantry and, excusing himself, left them to a game of chess.

"Who is he?" asked Mary when Lee had gone outside.

"I have no idea," said Allerton. Had he ever met Lee? He could not be sure. Formal introductions were not expected among the G.I. students. Was Lee a student? Allerton had never seen him at the school. There was nothing on the surface unusual in talking to someone you didn't know, but Lee put Allerton on guard. The man was somehow familiar to him. When Lee talked, he seemed to mean more than what he said. A special emphasis to a word or a greeting hinted at a period of familiarity in some other time and place. As though Lee were saying, "*You* know what I mean. *You* remember."

Allerton shrugged irritably and began arranging the chess pieces on the board. He looked like a sullen child unable to locate the source of his ill temper. After a few minutes of play his customary serenity returned, and he began humming.

It was after midnight when Lee returned to the Ship Ahoy. Drunks seethed around the bar, talking as if everyone else were stone deaf. Allerton stood on the edge of this group, apparently unable to make himself heard. He greeted Lee warmly, pushed into the bar, and emerged with two rum Cokes. "Let's sit down over here," he said.

Allerton was drunk. His eyes were flushed a faint violet tinge, the pupils widely dilated. He was talking very fast in a high, thin voice, the eerie, disembodied voice of a young child. Lee had never heard Allerton talk like this before. The effect was like the possession voice of a medium. The boy had an inhuman gaiety and innocence.

Allerton was telling a story about his experience with the Counter Intelligence Corps in Germany. An informant had been giving the department bum steers.

"How did you check the accuracy of information?" Lee asked. "How did you know ninety percent of what your informants told you wasn't fabricated?"

"Actually we didn't, and we got sucked in on a lot of phony deals. Of course, we cross-checked all information with other informants and we had our own agents in the field. Most of our informants turned in *some* phony information, but this one character made it all up. He had our agents out looking for a whole fictitious network of Russian spies. So finally the report comes back from Frankfurt—it is all a lot of crap. But instead of clearing out of town before the information could be checked, he came back with more.

"At this point we'd really had enough of his bullshit. So we locked him up in a cellar. The room was pretty cold and uncomfortable, but that was all we could do. We had to handle prisoners very careful. He kept typing out confessions, enormous things."

This story clearly delighted Allerton, and he kept laughing while he was telling it. Lee was impressed by his combination of intelligence and childlike charm. Allerton was friendly now, without reserve or defense, like a child who has never been hurt. He was telling another story.

Lee watched the thin hands, the beautiful violet eyes, the flush of excitement on the boy's face. An imaginary hand projected with such force it seemed Allerton must feel the touch of ectoplasmic fingers caressing his ear, phantom thumbs smoothing his eyebrows, pushing the hair back from his face. Now Lee's hands were running down over the ribs, the stomach. Lee felt the aching pain of desire in his lungs. His mouth was a little open, showing his teeth in the half snarl of a baffled animal. He licked his lips.

Lee did not enjoy frustration. The limitations of his desires were like the bars of a cage, like a chain and collar, something he had learned as an animal learns, through days and years of experiencing the snub of the chain, the unyielding bars. He had never resigned himself, and his eyes looked out through the invisible bars, watchful, alert, waiting for the keeper to forget the door, for the frayed collar, the loosened bar . . . suffering without despair and without consent.

"I went to the door and there he was with a branch in his mouth," Allerton was saying.

Lee had not been listening. "A branch in his mouth," said Lee, then added inanely, "A big branch?"

"It was about two feet long. I told him to drop dead, then a few minutes later he appeared at the window. So I threw a chair at him and he jumped down to the yard from the balcony. About eighteen feet. He was very nimble. Almost inhuman. It was sort of uncanny, and that's why I threw the chair. I was scared. We all figured he was putting on an act to get out of the army."

"What did he look like?" Lee asked.

"Look like? I don't remember especially. He was around eighteen. He looked like a clean-cut boy. We threw a bucket of cold water on him and left him on a cot downstairs. He began flopping around but he didn't say anything. We all decided that was an appropriate punishment. I think they took him to the hospital next day."

"Pneumonia?"

"I don't know. Maybe we shouldn't have thrown water on him."

Lee left Allerton at the door of his building.

"You go in here?" Lee asked.

"Yes, I have a sack here."

Lee said good night and walked home.

After that, Lee met Allerton every day at five in the Ship Ahoy. Allerton was accustomed to choose his friends from people older than himself, and he looked forward to meeting Lee. Lee had conversation routines that Allerton had never heard. But Allerton felt at times oppressed by Lee, as though Lee's presence shut off everything else. He thought he was seeing too much of Lee.

Allerton disliked commitments and had never been in love or had a close friend. He was forced to ask himself: "What does he want from me?" It did not occur to him that Lee was queer, as he associated queerness with at least some degree of overt effeminacy. Allerton was intelligent and surprisingly perceptive for a person so self-centered, but his experience was limited. He decided finally that Lee valued him as an audience.

CHAPTER 3

I t was a beautiful, clear afternoon in April. Punctually at five, Lee walked into the Ship Ahoy. Allerton was at the bar with Al Hyman, a periodic alcoholic and one of the nastiest, stupidest, dullest drunks Lee had ever known. He was, on the other hand, intelligent and simple in manner, and nice enough when sober. He was sober now.

Lee had a yellow scarf around his neck and a pair of two-peso dark glasses. He took off the scarf and glasses, and dropped them on the bar. "A hard day at the studio," he said, in affected theatrical accents. He ordered a rum Coke. "You know, it looks like we might bring in an oil well. They're drilling now over in quadrangle four, and from that rig you could almost spit over into Tex-Mex where I got my hundred-acre cotton farm."

"I always wanted to be an oil man," Hyman said.

Lee looked him over and shook his head. "I'm afraid not. You see, it isn't everybody can qualify. You must have the calling. First thing, you must look like an oil man. There are no young oil men. An oil man should be about fifty. His skin is cracked and wrinkled like mud that has dried in the sun, and especially the back of his neck is wrinkled, and the wrinkles are generally full of dust from looking over blocks and quadrangles. He wears gabardine slacks and a white short-sleeved sport shirt. His shoes are covered with fine dust, and a faint haze of dust follows him everywhere like a personal dust storm.

"So you got the calling and the proper appearance. You go around taking up leases. You get five or six people lined up to lease you their land for drilling. You go to the bank and talk to the president: 'Now Clem Farris, as fine a man as there is in this valley and smart too, he's in this thing up to his balls, and Old Man Scranton and Fred Crockly and Roy Spigot and Ted Bane, all of them good old boys. Now let me show you a few facts. I could set here and gas all morning, taking up your time, but I know you're a man accustomed to deal in facts and figures, and that's exactly what I'm here to show you.'

"He goes out to his car, always a coupe or a roadster— never saw an oil man with a sedan—and reaches in back of the seat and gets out his maps, a huge bundle of maps big as carpets. He spreads them out on the bank president's desk, and great clouds of dust spring up from the maps and fill the bank.

"'You see this quadrangle here? That's Tex-Mex. Now there's a fault runs right along here through Jed Marvin's place. I saw Old Jed too, the other day when I was out there, a good old boy. There isn't a finer man in this valley than Jed Marvin. Well now, Socony drilled right over here.'

"He spreads out more maps. He pulls over another desk and anchors the maps down with cuspidors. 'Well, they brought in a dry hole, and this map . . .' He unrolls another one. 'Now if you'll kindly sit on the other end so it don't roll up on us, I'll show you exactly why it was a dry hole and why they should never have drilled there in the first place, 'cause you can see just where this here fault runs smack between Jed's artesian well and the Tex-Mex line over into quadrangle four. Now that block was surveyed last time in 1922. I guess you know the old boy done the job. Earl Hoot was his name, a good old boy too. He had his home up in Nacogdoches, but his son-in-law owned a place down here, the old Brooks place up north of Tex-Mex, just across the line from . . .'

"By this time the president is punchy with boredom, and the dust is getting down in his lungs—oil men are constitutionally immune to the effects of dust—so he says, 'Well, if it's good enough for those boys, I guess it's good enough for me. I'll go along.'

"So the oil man goes back and pulls the same routine on his prospects. Then he gets a geologist down from Dallas or somewhere, who talks some gibberish about faults and seepage and intrusions and shale and sand, and selects someplace, more or less at random, to start drilling.

"Now the driller. He has to be a real rip-snorting character. They look for him in Boy's Town—the whore district in border towns—and they find him in a room full of empty bottles with three whores. So they bust a bottle over his head and drag him out and sober him up, and he looks at the drilling site and spits and says, 'Well, it's your hole.'

"Now if the well turns out dry, the oil man says, 'Well, that's the way it goes. Some holes got lubrication and some is dry as a whore's cunt on Sunday morning.' There was one oil man, Dry Hole Dutton they called him—all right, Allerton, no cracks about Vaseline—brought in twenty dry holes before he got cured. That means 'get rich,' in the salty lingo of the oil fraternity."

Joe Guidry came in, and Lee slid off his stool to shake hands. He was hoping Joe would bring up the subject of queerness so he could gauge Allerton's reaction. He figured it was time to let Allerton know what the score was. Such a thing as playing it too cool.

They sat down at a table. Somebody had stolen Guidry's radio, his riding boots, and his wristwatch. "The trouble with me is," said Guidry, "I like the type that robs me."

"Where you make your mistake is bringing them to your apartment," Lee said. "That's what hotels are for."

"You're right there. But half the time I don't have money for a hotel. Besides, I like someone around to cook breakfast and sweep the place out."

"*Clean* the place out."

"I don't mind the watch and the radio, but it really hurt, losing those boots. They were a thing of beauty and a joy forever." Guidry leaned forward and glanced at Allerton. "I don't know whether I ought to say things like this in front of Junior here. No offense, kid."

"Go ahead," said Allerton.

"Did I tell you how I made the cop on the beat? He's the *vigilante*, the watchman out where I live. Every time he sees the light on in my room, he comes in for a shot of rum. Well, about five nights ago he caught me when I was drunk and horny, and one thing led to another and I ended up showing him how the cow ate the cabbage. . . .

"So the night after I make him I was walking by the beer joint on the corner and he comes out *borracho* and says, 'Have a drink.' I said, 'I don't want a drink.' So he takes out his *pistola* and says, 'Have a drink.' I proceeded to take his *pistola* away from him, and he goes into the beer joint to phone for reinforcements. So I had to go in and rip the phone off the wall. Now they're billing me for the phone. When I got back to my room, which is on the ground floor, he had written '*El Puto Gringo*' on the window with soap. So instead of wiping it off, I left it there. It pays to advertise."

The drinks kept coming. Allerton went to the W.C. and got in a conversation at the bar. Guidry was accusing Hyman of being queer and pretending not to be. Lee was trying to explain to Guidry that Hyman wasn't really queer, and Guidry said to him, "He's queer and you aren't, Lee. You just go around pretending you're queer to get in on the act."

"Who wants to get in on your tired old act?" Lee said. He saw Allerton at the bar talking to John Dumé. Dumé belonged to a small clique of queers who made their headquarters in a beer joint on Campeche called The Green Lantern. Dumé himself was not an obvious queer, but the other Green Lantern boys were screaming fags who would not have been welcome at the Ship Ahoy.

Lee walked over to the bar and started talking to the bartender. He thought, "I hope Dumé tells him about me." Lee felt uncomfortable in dramatic something-I-have-to-tell-you routines and he knew, from unnerving experience, the difficulties of a casual come-on: "I'm queer, you know, by the way." Sometimes they don't hear right and yell, "What?" Or you toss in: "If you were as queer as I am." The other yawns and changes the subject, and you don't know whether he understood or not.

The bartender was saying, "She asks me why I drink. What can I tell her? I don't know why. Why did you have the monkey on your back? Do you know why? There isn't any why, but try to explain that to someone like Jerry. Try to explain that to any woman." Lee nodded sympathetically. "She says to me, why don't you get more sleep and eat better? She don't understand and I can't explain it. Nobody can explain it."

The bartender moved away to wait on some customers. Dumé came over to Lee. "How do you like this character?" he said, indicating Allerton with a wave of his beer bottle. Allerton was across the room talking to Mary and a chess player from Peru. "He comes to me and says, 'I thought you were one of the Green Lantern boys.' So I said, 'Well, I am.' He wants me to take him around to some of the gay places here."

Lee and Allerton went to see Cocteau's *Orpheus*. In the dark theater Lee could feel his body pull toward Allerton, an amoeboid protoplasmic projection, straining with a blind worm hunger to enter the other's body, to breathe with his lungs, see with his eyes, learn the feel of his viscera and genitals. Allerton shifted in his seat. Lee felt a sharp twinge, a strain or dislocation of the spirit. His eyes ached. He took off his glasses and ran his hand over his closed eyes.

When they left the theater, Lee felt exhausted. He fumbled and bumped into things. His voice was toneless with strain. He put his hand up to his head from time to time, an awkward, involuntary gesture of pain. "I need a drink," he said. He pointed to a bar across the street. "There," he said.

He sat down in a booth and ordered a double tequila. Allerton ordered rum and Coke. Lee drank the tequila straight down, listening down into himself for the effect. He ordered another.

"What did you think of the picture?" Lee asked.

"Enjoyed parts of it."

"Yes." Lee nodded, pursing his lips and looking down into his empty glass. "So did I." He pronounced the words very carefully, like an elocution teacher.

"He always gets some innaresting effects." Lee laughed. Euphoria was spreading from his stomach. He drank half the second tequila. "The innaresting thing about Cocteau is his ability to bring the myth alive in modern terms."

"Ain't it the truth?" said Allerton.

They went to a Russian restaurant for dinner. Lee looked through the menu. "By the way," he said, "the law was in, putting the bite on the Ship Ahoy again. Vice squad. Two hundred pesos. I can see them in the station house after a hard day shaking down citizens of the Federal District. One cop says, 'Ah, Gonzalez, you should see what I got today. Oh la la, such a bite!'

"'Aah, you shook down a *puto* queer for two pesetas in a bus station crapper. We know you, Hernandez, and your cheap tricks. You're the cheapest cop inna Federal District.'"

Lee waved to the waiter. "Hey, Jack. *Dos* martinis, much dry. *Seco.* And *dos* plates Sheeshka Babe. *Sabe?*"

The waiter nodded. "That's two dry martinis and two orders of shish kebab. Right, gentlemen?"

"Solid, Pops. . . . So how was your evening with Dumé?" Lee said.

"We went to several bars full of queers. One place a character asked me to dance and propositioned me."

"Take him up?"

"No."

"Dumé is a nice fellow."

Allerton smiled. "Yes, but he is not a person I would confide too much in. That is, anything I wanted to keep private."

"You refer to a specific indiscretion?"

"Frankly, yes."

"I see." Lee thought, "Dumé never misses."

The waiter put two martinis on the table. Lee held his martini up to the candle, looking at it with distaste. "The inevitable watery martini with a decomposing olive," he said.

Lee bought a lottery ticket from a boy of ten or so, who had rushed in when the waiter went to the kitchen. The boy was working the last-ticket routine. Lee paid him expansively, like a drunk American. "Go buy yourself some marijuana, son," he said. The boy smiled and turned to leave. "Come back in five years and make an easy ten pesos," Lee called after him.

Allerton smiled. "Thank God," Lee thought. "I won't have to contend with middle-class morality."

"Here you are, sir," said the waiter, placing the shish kebab on the table.

Lee ordered two glasses of red wine. "So Dumé told you about my, uh, proclivities?" he said abruptly.

"Yes," said Allerton, his mouth full.

"A curse," said Lee. "Been in our family for generations. The Lees have always been perverts. I shall never forget the unspeakable horror that froze the lymph in my glands—the lymph glands that is, of course—when the baneful word seared my reeling brain: *homosexual*. I was a homosexual. I thought of the painted, simpering female impersonators I had seen in a Baltimore night club. Could it be possible that I was one of those subhuman things? I walked the streets in a daze, like a man with a light concussion—just a minute, Doctor Kildare, this isn't your script. I might well have destroyed myself, ending an existence which seemed to offer nothing but grotesque misery and humiliation. Nobler, I thought, to die a man than live on, a sex monster. It was a wise old queen—Bobo, we called her—who taught me that I had a duty to live and to bear my burden proudly for all to see, to conquer prejudice and ignorance and hate with knowledge and sincerity and love. Whenever you are threatened by a hostile presence, you emit a thick cloud of love like an octopus squirts out ink.

"Poor Bobo came to a sticky end. He was riding in the Duc de Ventre's Hispano-Suiza when his falling piles blew out of the car and wrapped around the rear wheel. He was completely gutted, leaving an empty shell sitting there on the giraffe-skin upholstery. Even the eyes and the brain went, with a horrible slupping sound. The Duc says he will carry that ghastly slup with him to his mausoleum.

"Then I knew the meaning of loneliness. But Bobo's words came back to me from the tomb, the sibilants cracking gently. 'No one is ever really alone. You are part of everything alive.' The difficulty is to convince someone else he is really part of you, so what the hell? Us parts ought to work together. Reet?"

Lee paused, looking at Allerton speculatively. "Just where do I stand with the kid?" he wondered. Allerton had listened politely, smiling at intervals. "What I mean is, Allerton, we are all parts of a tremendous whole. No use fighting it." Lee was getting tired of the routine. He looked around restlessly for some place to put it down. "Don't these gay bars depress you? Of course, the queer bars here aren't to compare with stateside queer joints."

"I wouldn't know," said Allerton. "I've never been in any queer joints except those Dumé took me to. I guess there's kicks and kicks."

"You haven't, really?"

"No, never."

Lee paid the bill and they walked out into the cool

night. A crescent moon was clear and green in the sky. They walked aimlessly.

"Shall we go to my place for a drink? I have some Napoleon brandy."

"All right," said Allerton.

"This is a completely unpretentious little brandy, you understand, none of this tourist treacle with obvious effects of flavoring, appealing to the mass tongue. My brandy has no need of shoddy devices to shock and coerce the palate. Come along." Lee called a cab.

"Three pesos to Insurgentes and Monterrey," Lee said to the driver in his atrocious Spanish. The driver said four. Lee waved him on. The driver muttered something and opened the door.

Inside, Lee turned to Allerton. "The man plainly harbors subversive thoughts. You know, when I was at Princeton, Communism was the thing. To come out flat for private property and a class society, you marked yourself a stupid lout or suspect to be a High Episcopalian pederast. But I held out against the infection—of Communism I mean, of course."

"*Aquí*," said Lee. He handed the driver three pesos. The driver muttered some more and started the car with a vicious clash of gears.

"Sometimes I think they don't like us," said Allerton.

"I don't mind people disliking me," Lee said. "The question is, what are they in a position to do about it? Apparently nothing, at present. They don't have the green light. This driver, for example, hates gringos. But if he kills someone—and very possibly he will—it will not be an

American. It will be another Mexican. Maybe his good friend. Friends are less frightening than strangers."

Lee opened the door of his apartment and turned on the light. Lee's apartment was pervaded by seemingly hopeless disorder. Here and there, ineffectual attempts had been made to arrange things in piles. There were no lived-in touches. No pictures, no decorations. Clearly, none of the furniture was his. But Lee's presence permeated the apartment. A coat over the back of a chair and a hat on the table were immediately recognizable as belonging to Lee.

"I'll fix you a drink." Lee got two water glasses from the kitchen and poured two inches of Mexican brandy in each glass.

Allerton tasted the brandy. "Good Lord," he said. "Napoleon must have pissed in this one."

"I was afraid of that. An untutored palate. Your generation has never learned the pleasures that a trained palate confers on the disciplined few."

Lee took a long drink of the brandy. He attempted an ecstatic "aah," inhaled some of the brandy, and began to cough. "It *is* god-awful," he said when he could talk. "Still, better than California brandy. It has a suggestion of cognac taste."

There was a long silence. Allerton was sitting with his head leaning back against the couch. His eyes were half-closed.

"Can I show you over the house?" said Lee, standing up. "In here we have the bedroom."

Allerton got to his feet slowly. They went into the bedroom, and Allerton lay down on the bed and lit a cigarette. Lee sat in the only chair.

"More brandy?" Lee asked. Allerton nodded. Lee sat down on the edge of the bed and filled Allerton's glass and handed it to him. Lee touched his sweater. "Sweet stuff, dearie," he said. "That wasn't made in Mexico."

"I bought it in Scotland," said Allerton. He began to hiccough violently. He got up and rushed for the bathroom.

Lee stood in the doorway. "Too bad," he said. "What could be the matter? You didn't drink much." He filled a glass with water and handed it to Allerton. "You all right now?" he asked.

"Yes, I think so." Allerton lay down on the bed again.

Lee reached out a hand and touched Allerton's ear and caressed the side of his face. Allerton reached up and covered one of Lee's hands and squeezed it.

"Let's get this sweater off."

"O.K.," said Allerton. He took off the sweater and then lay down again.

Lee took off his own shoes and shirt. He opened Allerton's shirt and ran his hand down the ribs and the stomach, which contracted beneath his fingers. "God, you're skinny," he said.

"I'm pretty small."

Lee took off Allerton's shoes and socks. He loosened Allerton's belt and unbuttoned his trousers. Allerton arched his body, and Lee pulled the trousers and drawers off. He dropped his own trousers and shorts and lay down beside him. Allerton responded without hostility or disgust, but in his eyes Lee saw a curious detachment, the impersonal calm of an animal or a child.

Later, when they lay side by side smoking, Lee said, "Oh, by the way, you said you had a camera in pawn you were about to lose?" It occurred to Lee that to bring the matter up at this time was not tactful, but he decided the other was not the type to take offense.

"Yes. In for four hundred pesos. The ticket runs out next Wednesday."

"Well, let's go down tomorrow and get it out."

Allerton raised one bare shoulder off the sheet. "O.K.," he said.

CHAPTER 4

Friday night Allerton went to work. He was taking his roommate's place proofreading for an English newspaper.

Saturday night Lee met Allerton for dinner in the Cuba, a bar with an interior like the set for a surrealist ballet. The walls were covered with murals depicting underwater scenes. Mermaids and mermen in elaborate arrangements with huge goldfish stared at the customers with fixed, identical expressions of pathic dismay. Even the fish were invested with an air of ineffectual alarm. The effect was disquieting, as though these androgynous beings were frightened by something behind or to one side of the customers, who were made uneasy by this inferred presence. Most of them took their business someplace else.

Allerton was somewhat sullen, and Lee felt depressed and ill at ease until he had put down two martinis. "You know, Allerton . . . ," he said after a long silence. Allerton was humming to himself, drumming on the table, and looking around restlessly. Allerton stopped humming and raised an eyebrow.

"This punk is getting too smart," Lee thought. He knew he had no way of punishing Allerton for indifference or insolence.

"They have the most incompetent tailors in Mexico I have encountered in all my experience as a traveler. Have you had any work done?" He looked pointedly at Allerton's shabby clothes. Allerton was as careless of his clothes as Lee was. "Apparently not. Take this tailor I'm hung up with. Simple job. I bought a pair of ready-made trousers. Never took time for a fitting. Both of us could get in those pants."

"It wouldn't look right," said Allerton.

"People would think we were Siamese twins. Did I ever tell you about the Siamese twin who turned his brother in to the law to get him off the junk? But to get back to this tailor. I took the pants in with another pair. 'These pants is too voluminous,' I told him. 'I want them sewed down to the same size as this other pair here.' He promised to do the job in two days. That was more than two months ago. '*Mañana*,' '*Más tarde*,' '*Ahora*,' '*Ahorita*,' and every time I come to pick up the pants it's '*todavía no*'—not yet. Yesterday I had all the *ahora* routine I can stand still for. So I told him, 'Ready or no, give me my pants.' The pants was all cut down the seams. I told him, 'Two months and all you have done is disembowel my trousers.' I took them to another tailor and told him, 'Sew them up.' Are you hungry?"

"I am, as a matter of fact."

"How about Pat's Steak House?"

"Good idea."

Pat's served excellent steaks. Lee liked the place because it was never crowded. At Pat's he ordered a double dry martini. Allerton had rum and Coke. Lee began talking about telepathy.

"I know telepathy to be a fact, since I have experienced it myself. I have no interest to prove it, or, in fact, to prove anything to anybody. What interests me is, how can I use it? In South America at the headwaters of the Amazon grows a plant called Yage that is supposed to increase telepathic sensitivity. Medicine men use it in their work. A Colombian scientist, whose name escapes me, isolated from Yage a drug he called Telepathine. I read all this in a magazine article.

"Later I see another article: the Russians are using Yage in experiments on slave labor. It seems they want to induce states of automatic obedience and ultimately, of course, 'thought control.' The basic con. No buildup, no spiel, no routine, just move in on someone's psyche and give orders. I have a theory the Mayan priests developed a form of one-way telepathy to con the peasants into doing all the work. The deal is certain to backfire eventually, because telepathy is not of its nature a one-way setup, nor a setup of sender and receiver at all.

"By now the U.S. is experimenting with Yage, unless they are dumber even than I think. Yage might be a means to usable knowledge of telepathy. Anything that can be accomplished chemically can be accomplished in other ways." Lee saw that Allerton was not especially interested, and dropped the subject.

"Did you read about the old Jew who tried to smuggle out ten pounds of gold sewed in his overcoat?"

"No. What about it?"

"Well, this old Jew was nailed at the airport on his way to Cuba. I hear they got like a mine finder out at the airport rings a bell if anybody passes the gate with an outlandish quantity of metal on his person. So it says in the papers, after they give this Jew a shake and find the gold, a large number of Jewish-looking foreigners were seen looking into the airport window in a state of excitement. 'Oy, gefilte fish! They are putting the snatch on Abe!' Back in Roman times the Jews rose up—in Jerusalem I think it was—and killed fifty thousand Romans. The she-Jews—ah, that is, the young Jewish ladies, I must be careful not to lay myself open to a charge of anti-Semitism—done strip teases with Roman intestines.

"Speaking of intestines, did I ever tell you about my friend Reggie? One of the unsung heroes of British Intelligence. Lost his ass and ten feet of lower intestine in the service. Lived for years disguised as an Arab boy known only as 'Number 69' at headquarters. That was wistful thinking, though, because the Arabs are strictly one-way. Well, a rare Oriental disease set in, and poor Reggie lost the bulk of his tripes. For God and country, what? He didn't want any speeches, any medals, just to *know* that he had served, that was enough. Think of those patient years, waiting for another piece of the jigsaw puzzle to fall into place.

"You never hear of operators like Reggie, but it is their information, gathered in pain and danger, that gives some frontline general the plan for a brilliant counter-offensive and covers his chest with medals. For example, Reggie was the first to learn the enemy was running short of petrol when the K-Y gave out, and that was only one of his brilliant coups. How about the T-bone steak for two?"

"That's fine."

"Rare?"

"Medium rare."

Lee was looking at the menu. "They list baked Alaska," he said. "Ever eat it?"

"No."

"Real good. Hot on the outside and cold inside."

"That's why they call it baked Alaska, I imagine."

"Got an idea for a new dish. Take a live pig and throw it into a very hot oven so the pig is roasted outside and, when you cut into it, still alive and twitching inside. Or, if we run a dramatic joint, a screaming pig covered with burning brandy rushes out of the kitchen and dies right by your chair. You can reach down and pull off the crispy, crackly ears and eat them with your cocktails."

Outside, the city lay under a violet haze. A warm spring wind blew through the trees in the park. They walked through the park back to Lee's place, occasionally stopping to lean against each other, weak from laughing. A Mexican said, "*Cabrones*," as he walked by. Lee called after him, "*Chinga tu madre*," then added in English, "Here I come to your little jerkwater country and spend my good American dollars and what happens? Insulted inna public street." The Mexican turned, hesitating. Lee unbuttoned his coat and hooked his thumb under the pistol at his waistband. The Mexican walked on.

"Someday they won't walk away," said Lee.

At Lee's apartment they had some brandy. Lee put his arm around Allerton's shoulder.

"Well, if you insist," said Allerton.

Sunday night Allerton had dinner at Lee's apartment. Lee cooked chicken livers, because Allerton always wanted to order chicken liver in restaurants, and usually restaurant chicken liver isn't fresh. After dinner Lee began making love to Allerton, but he rejected Lee's advances and said he wanted to go to the Ship Ahoy and drink a rum Coke. Lee turned out the light and embraced Allerton before they started out the door. Allerton's body was rigid with annoyance.

When they arrived at the Ship Ahoy, Lee went to the bar and ordered two rum Cokes. "Make those extra strong," he said to the bartender.

Allerton was sitting at a table with Mary. Lee brought the rum Coke over and set it down by Allerton. Then he sat down at a table with Joe Guidry. Guidry had a young man with him. The young man was telling how he was treated by an army psychiatrist. "So what did you find out from your psychiatrist?" said Guidry. His voice had a nagging, derogatory edge.

"I found out I was an Oedipus. I found out I love my mother."

"Why, everybody loves their mother, son," said Guidry.

"I mean I love my mother physically."

"I don't believe that, son," said Guidry. This struck Lee as funny, and he began to laugh.

"I hear Jim Cochan has gone back to the States," said Guidry. "He plans to work in Alaska."

"Thank God I am a gentleman of independent means and don't have to expose myself to the inclemencies of near-Arctic conditions," said Lee. "By the way, did you ever meet Jim's wife, Alice? My God, she is an American bitch that won't quit. I never yet see her equal. Jim does not have one friend he can take to the house. She has forbidden him to eat out, as she does not want he should take in any nourishment unless she is there to watch him eat it. Did you ever hear the likes of that? Needless to say, my place is out of bounds to Jim, and he always has that hunted look when he comes to see me. I don't know why American men put up with such shit from a woman. Of course I am no expert judge of female flesh, but Alice has 'lousy lay' writ all over her scrawny, unappetizing person."

"You're coming on mighty bitchy tonight, Lee," said Guidry.

"And not without reason. Did I tell you about this Wigg person? He is an American hipster around town, a junky who is said to play a cool bass fiddle. Strictly on the chisel, even though he has gold, and he's always mooching junk, saying, 'No, I don't want to *buy* any. I'm kicking. I just want half a fix.' I have had all I can stand still for from this character. Driving around in a new three-thousand-dollar Chrysler and too cheap to buy his own junk. What am I, the Junky's Benevolent Society for Chrissakes? This Wigg is as ugly as people get."

"You making it with him?" asked Guidry, which seemed to shock his young friend.

"Not even. I got bigger fish to fry," said Lee. He glanced over at Allerton, who was laughing at something Mary had said.

"Fish is right," quipped Guidry. "Cold, slippery, and hard to catch."

CHAPTER 5

L ee had an appointment with Allerton for eleven o'clock Monday morning to go to the National Pawn Shop and get his camera out of hock. Lee came to Allerton's room and woke him up exactly at eleven. Allerton was sullen. He seemed on the point of going back to sleep. Finally Lee said, "Well, are you going to get up now, or . . ."

Allerton opened his eyes and blinked like a turtle. "I'm getting up," he said.

Lee sat down and read a newspaper, careful to avoid watching Allerton dress. He was trying to control his hurt and anger, and the effort exhausted him. A heavy drag slowed movement and thought. His face was rigid, his voice toneless. The strain continued through breakfast. Allerton sipped tomato juice in silence.

It took all day to get the camera. Allerton had lost the ticket. They went from one office to another. The officials shook their heads and drummed on the table, waiting. Lee put out two hundred pesos extra in bites. He finally paid the four hundred pesos, plus interest and various charges. He handed the camera to Allerton, who took it without comment.

They went back to the Ship Ahoy in silence. Lee went in and ordered a drink. Allerton disappeared. About an hour later he came in and sat with Lee.

"How about dinner tonight?" asked Lee.

Allerton said, "No, I think I'll work tonight."

Lee was depressed and shattered. The warmth and laughter of Saturday night was lost, and he did not know why. In any relation of love or friendship, Lee attempted to establish contact on the non-verbal level of intuition, a silent exchange of thought and feeling. Now Allerton had abruptly shut off contact, and Lee felt a physical pain, as though a part of himself tentatively stretched out toward the other had been severed, and he was looking at the bleeding stump in shock and disbelief.

Lee said, "Like the Wallace administration, I subsidize non-production. I will pay you twenty pesos not to work tonight." Lee was about to develop the idea, but Allerton's impatient coolness stopped him. He fell silent, looking at Allerton with shocked, hurt eyes.

Allerton was nervous and irritable, drumming on the table and looking around. He did not himself understand why Lee annoyed him.

"How about a drink?" Lee said.

"No. Not now. Anyway, I have to go."

Lee got up jerkily. "Well, I'll see you," he said. "I'll see you tomorrow."

"Yes. Good night."

He left Lee standing there, trying to formulate a plan to keep Allerton from going, to make an appointment for the next day, to mitigate in some way the hurt he had received.

Allerton was gone. Lee felt for the back of his chair and lowered himself into it, like a man weak from illness. He stared at the table, his thoughts slow, as if he were very cold.

The bartender placed a sandwich in front of him. "Huh?" said Lee. "What's this?"

"The sandwich you ordered."

"Oh, yes." Lee took a few bites out of the sandwich, washing it down with water. "On my bill, Joe," he called to the bartender.

He got up and walked out. He walked slowly. Several times he leaned on a tree, looking at the ground as if his stomach hurt. Inside his apartment he took off his coat and shoes, and sat down on the bed. His throat began to ache, moisture hit his eyes, and he fell across the bed, sobbing convulsively. He pulled his knees up and covered his face with his hands, the fists clenched. Toward morning he turned on his back and stretched out. The sobs stopped, and his face relaxed in the morning light.

Lee woke up around noon and sat for a long time on the edge of the bed, with one shoe dangling from his hand. He dabbed water on his eyes, put on his coat, and went out.

Lee went down to the Zócalo and wandered around for several hours. His mouth was dry. He went into a Chinese restaurant and sat down in a booth and ordered a Coke. Misery spread through his body now that he was sitting down with no motion to distract him. "What happened?"

He forced himself to look at the facts. Allerton was not queer enough to make a reciprocal relation possible. Lee's affection irritated him. Like many people who have nothing to do, he was very resentful of any claims on his time. He had no close friends. He disliked definite appointments. He did not like to feel that anybody expected anything from him. He wanted, so far as possible, to live without external pressure. Allerton resented Lee's action in paying to recover the camera. He felt he was "being sucked in on a phony deal" and that an obligation he did not want had been thrust upon him.

Allerton did not recognize friends who made six-hundred-peso gifts, nor could he feel comfortable exploiting Lee. He made no attempt to clarify the situation. He did not want to see the contradiction involved in resenting a favor which he accepted. Lee found that he could tune in on Allerton's viewpoint, though the process caused him pain, since it involved seeing the extent of Allerton's indifference. "I liked him and I wanted him to like me," Lee thought. "I wasn't trying to buy anything."

"I have to leave town," he decided. "Go somewhere. Panama, South America." He went down to the station to find out when the next train left for Veracruz. There was a train that night, but he did not buy a ticket. A feeling of cold desolation came over him at the thought of arriving alone in another country, far away from Allerton.

Lee took a cab to the Ship Ahoy. Allerton was not there, and Lee sat at the bar for three hours, drinking. Finally Allerton looked in the door, waved to Lee vaguely, and went upstairs with Mary. Lee knew they had probably gone to the owner's apartment, where they often ate dinner.

He went up to Tom Weston's apartment. Mary and Allerton were there. Lee sat down and tried to engage Allerton's interest, but he was too drunk to make sense. His attempt to carry on a casually humorous conversation was painful to watch.

He must have slept. Mary and Allerton were gone. Tom Weston brought him some hot coffee. He drank the coffee, got up, and staggered out of the apartment. Exhausted, he slept till the following morning.

Scenes from the chaotic, drunken month passed before his eyes. There was a face he did not recognize, a good-looking kid with amber eyes, yellow hair, and beautiful straight black eyebrows. He saw himself asking someone he barely knew to buy him a beer in a bar on Insurgentes, and getting a nasty brush. He saw himself pull a gun on someone who followed him out of a clip joint on Coahuila and tried to roll him. He felt the friendly, steadying hands of people who had helped him home. "Take it easy, Bill." His childhood friend Rollins standing there, solid and virile, with his elkhound. Carl running for a streetcar. Moor with his malicious bitch smile. The faces blended together in a nightmare, speaking to him in strange moaning idiot voices that he could not understand at first and finally could not hear.

Lee got up and shaved and felt better. He found he could eat a roll and drink some coffee. He smoked and read the paper, trying not to think about Allerton. Presently he went downtown and looked through the gun stores. He found a bargain in a Colt Frontier, which he bought for two hundred pesos. A .32-20 in perfect condition, serial number in the three hundred thousands. Worth at least a hundred dollars stateside.

Lee went to the American bookstore and bought a book on chess. He took the book out to Chapultepec, sat down in a soda stand on the lagoon, and began to read. Directly in front of him was an island with a huge cypress tree growing on it. Hundreds of vultures roosted in the tree. Lee wondered what they ate. He threw a piece of bread, which landed on the island. The vultures paid no attention.

Lee was interested in the Theory of Games and the strategy of random behavior. As he had supposed, the Theory of Games does not apply to chess, since chess rules out the element of chance and approaches elimination of the unpredictable human factor. If the mechanism of chess were completely understood, the outcome could be predicted after any initial move. "A game for thinking machines," Lee thought. He read on, smiling from time to time. Finally he got up, sailed the book out over the lagoon, and walked away.

Lee knew he could not find what he wanted with Allerton. The court of fact had rejected his petition. But Lee could not give up. "Perhaps I can discover a way to change fact," he thought. He was ready to take any risk, to proceed to any extreme of action. Like a saint or a wanted criminal with nothing to lose, Lee had stepped beyond the claims of his nagging, cautious, aging, frightened flesh.

He took a taxi to the Ship Ahoy. Allerton was standing in front of the Ship Ahoy, blinking sluggishly in the sunlight. Lee looked at him and smiled. Allerton smiled back.

"How are you?" said Lee.

"Sleepy. Just got up." He yawned and started into the Ship Ahoy. He moved one hand—"See you"—and sat at the bar and ordered tomato juice. Lee sat beside him and ordered a double rum Coke. Allerton moved and sat down at a table with the Westons. "Bring the tomato juice over here, will you, Joe?" he called to the bartender.

Lee sat at the table next to Allerton's. The Westons were leaving. Allerton followed them out. He came back in and sat in the other room, reading the papers. Mary came in and sat down with Allerton. After talking for a few minutes, they set up the chess board.

Lee had thrown down three drinks. He walked over and pulled up a chair to the table where Mary and Allerton were playing chess. "Howdy," he said. "Don't mind if I kibitz?"

Mary looked up annoyed, but smiled when she met Lee's steady, reckless gaze.

"I was reading up on chess. Arabs invented it, and I'm not surprised. Nobody can sit like an Arab. The classical

Arab chess game was simply a sitting contest. When both contestants starved to death, it was a stalemate." Lee paused and took a long drink.

"During the Baroque period of chess the practice of harrying your opponent with some annoying mannerism came into general use. Some players used dental floss, others cracked their joints or blew saliva bubbles. The method was constantly developed. In the 1917 match at Baghdad, the Arab Arachnid Khayam defeated the German master Kurt Schlemiel by humming 'I'll Be Around When You're Gone' forty thousand times, and each time reaching his hand toward the board as if he intended to make a move. Schlemiel went into convulsions finally.

"Did you ever have the good fortune to see the Italian master Tetrazzini perform?" Lee lit Mary's cigarette. "I say 'perform' advisedly, because he was a great showman and, like all showmen, not above charlatanism and at times downright trickery. Sometimes he used smoke screens to hide his maneuvers from the opposition—I mean literal smoke screens, of course. He had a corps of trained idiots who would rush in at a given signal and eat all the pieces. With defeat staring him in the face—as it often did, because actually he knew nothing of chess but the rules and wasn't too sure of those—he would leap up yelling, 'You cheap bastard! I saw you palm that queen!' and ram a broken teacup into his opponent's face. In 1922 he was rid out of Prague on a rail. The next time I saw Tetrazzini was in the Upper Ubangi. A complete wreck. Peddling unlicensed condoms. That was the year of the rinderpest, when everything died, even the hyenas."

Lee paused. The routine was coming to him like dictation. He did not know what he was going to say next, but
he suspected the monologue was about to get dirty. He
looked at Mary. She was exchanging significant glances
with Allerton. "Some sort of lover code," Lee decided. "She
is telling him they have to go now." Allerton got up, saying
he had to have a haircut before going to work. Mary and
Allerton left. Lee was alone in the bar.

The monologue continued. "I was working as Aide-de-
camp under General Von Klutch. Exacting. A hard man to
satisfy. I gave up trying after the first week. We had a saying
around the wardroom: 'Never expose your flank to old
Klutchy.' Well, I couldn't take Klutchy another night, so I
assembled a modest caravan and hit the trail with Abdul,
the local Adonis. Ten miles out of Tanhajaro, Abdul came
down with the rinderpest and I had to leave him there to
die. Hated to do it, but there was no other way. Lost his
looks completely, you understand.

"At the headwaters of the Zambesi, I ran into an old
Dutch trader. After considerable haggling I gave him a keg
of paregoric for a boy, half Effendi and half Lulu. I figured
the boy would get me as far as Timbuktu, maybe all the
way to Dakar. But the Lulu-Effendi was showing signs of
wear even before I hit Timbuktu, and I decided to trade
him in on a straight Bedouin model. The crossbreeds make
a good appearance, but they don't hold up. In Timbuktu I
went to Corn Hole Gus's Used-Slave Lot to see what he
could do for me on a trade-in.

"Gus rushes out and goes into the spiel: 'Ah, Sahib
Lee. Allah has sent you! I have something right up your

ass, I mean, alley. Just came in. One owner and he was a
doctor. A once-over-lightly, twice-a-week-type citizen.
It's young and it's tender. In fact, it talks baby talk. . . .
Behold!'

"'You call those senile slobberings baby talk? My
grandfather got a clap off that one. Come again, Gussie.'

"'You do not like it? A pity. Well, everyone has a taste,
feller say. Now, here I have a one-hundred-percent-desert-
bred Bedouin with a pedigree goes straight back to the
Prophet. Dig his bearing. Such pride! Such fire!'

"'A good appearance job, Gus, but not good enough.
It's an albino Mongolian idiot. Look, Gussie, you are dealing with the oldest faggot in the Upper Ubangi, so come
off the peg. Reach down into your grease pit and dredge
out the best-looking punk you got in this moth-eaten
bazaar.'

"'All right, Sahib Lee. You want quality, right? Follow
me, please. Here it is. What can I say? Quality speaks for
itself. Now, I got a lotta cheap-type customers in here
wanta see quality and then scream at the price. But you
know and I know that quality runs high. As a matter of fact,
and this I swear by the Prophet's prick, I lose money on this
quality merchandise.'

"'Uh-huh. Got some hidden miles on him, but he'll
do. How about a trial run?'

"'Lee, for Chrissake, I don't run a house. This joint is
strictly package. No consumption on premises. I could lose
my license.'

"'I don't aim to get caught short with one of your
Scotch-tape-and-household-cement reconditioned jobs a

hundred miles from the nearest souk. Besides, how do I know it ain't a Liz?'

"'Sahib Lee! This is an ethical lot!'

"'I was beat that way one time in Marrakesh. Citizen passed a transvestite Jew Lizzie on me as an Abyssinian prince.'

"'Ha-ha-ha. Full of funny jokes, aren't you? How is this: stay over in town tonight and try it out. If you don't want it in the morning, I refund every piaster. Fair enough?'

"'O.K. Now, what can you give me on this Lulu-Effendi? Perfect condition. Just overhauled. He don't eat much and he don't say nothing.'

"'Jesus, Lee! You know I'd cut off my right nut for you, but I swear by my mother's cunt, may I fall down and be paralyzed and my prick fall off if these mixed jobs ain't harder to move than a junky's bowels.'

"'Skip the routine. How much?'

"Gus stands in front of the Lulu-Effendi with his hands on his hips. He smiles and shakes his head. He walks around the boy. He reaches in and points to a small, slightly varicose vein behind the knee. 'Look at that,' he says, still smiling and shaking his head. He walks around again. . . . 'Got piles too.' He shakes his head. 'I don't know. I really don't know what to say to you. Open up, kid. . . . Two teeth missing.' Gus has stopped smiling. He is talking in low, considerate tones, like an undertaker.

"'I'm going to be honest with you, Lee. I've got a lot full of this mixed stuff now. I'd rather just forget this job and talk cash on the other.'

"'What am I going to do with it? Peddle it on the public street?'

"'Might take it along as a spare. Ha-ha . . .'

"'Ha. What can you give me?'

"'Well . . . now don't get mad . . . two hundred piasters.' He makes a skittish little run, as if to escape my anger, and throws up a huge cloud of dust in the courtyard."

The routine ended suddenly, and Lee looked around. The bar was nearly empty. He paid for his drinks and walked out into the night.

CHAPTER 6

Thursday Lee went to the races, on the recommendation of Tom Weston. Weston was an amateur astrologer, and he assured Lee the signs were right. Lee lost five races and took a taxi back to the Ship Ahoy.

Mary and Allerton were sitting at a table with the Peruvian chess player. Allerton asked Lee to come over and sit down at the table.

"Where's that phony whore caster?" Lee said, looking around.

"Tom give you a bum steer?" asked Allerton.

"He did that."

Mary left with the Peruvian. Lee finished his third drink and turned to Allerton. "I figure to go down to South America soon," he said. "Why don't you come along? Won't cost you a cent."

"Perhaps not in money."

"I'm not a difficult man to get along with," said Lee. "We could reach a satisfactory arrangement. What you got to lose?"

"Independence."

"So who's going to cut in on your independence? You can lay all the women in South America if you want to. All I ask is be nice to Papa, say twice a week. That isn't excessive, is it? Besides, I will buy you a round-trip ticket so you can leave at your discretion."

Allerton shrugged. "I'll think it over," he said. "This job runs ten days more. I'll give you a definite answer when the job folds."

"Your job. . . ." Lee was about to say, "I'll give you ten days' salary." He said, "All right."

Allerton's newspaper job was temporary, and he was too lazy to hold a job in any case. Consequently his answer meant "No." Lee figured to talk him over in ten days. "Better not force the issue now," he thought.

Allerton planned a three-day trip to Morelia with his co-workers in the newspaper office. The night before Allerton left, Lee was in a state of manic excitement. He collected a noisy table full of people. Allerton was playing chess with Mary, and Lee made all the noise he could. He kept his table laughing, but they all looked vaguely uneasy, as if they would prefer to be someplace else. They thought Lee was a little crazy. But just when he seemed on the point of some scandalous excess of speech or behavior, he would check himself and say something completely banal.

Lee leaped up to embrace a new arrival. "Ricardo! *Amigo mío!*" he said. "Haven't seen you in a dog's age. Where you been? Having a baby? Sit down on your ass, or what's left of it after four years in the navy. . . . What's troubling you, Richard? Is it women? I'm glad you came to me instead of those quacks on the top floor."

At this point Allerton and Mary left, after consulting for a moment in low tones. Lee looked after them in silence. "I'm playing to an empty house now," he thought. He ordered another rum and swallowed four Benzedrine tablets. Then he went into the head and smoked a roach of tea. "Now I will ravish my public," he thought.

The busboy had caught a mouse and was holding it up by the tail. Lee pulled out an old-fashioned .22 revolver he sometimes carried. "Hold the son of a bitch out and I'll blast it," he said, striking a Napoleonic pose. The boy tied a string to the mouse's tail and held it out at arm's length. Lee fired from a distance of three feet. His bullet tore the mouse's head off.

"If you'd got any closer, the mouse would have clogged the muzzle," said Richard.

Tom Weston came in. "Here comes the old whore caster," said Lee. "That retrograde Saturn dragging your ass, man?"

"My ass is dragging because I need a beer," said Weston.

"Well, you've come to the right place. A beer for my astrologizing friend. . . . What's that? I'm sorry, old man," Lee said, turning to Weston, "but the bartender says the signs aren't right to serve you a beer. You see, Venus is in the sixty-ninth house with a randy Neptune and he couldn't let you have a beer under such auspices." Lee washed down a small piece of opium with black coffee.

Horace walked in and gave Lee his brief, cold nod. Lee rushed over and embraced him. "This thing is bigger than both of us, Horace," he said. "Why hide our love?"

Horace thrust out his arms rigidly. "Knock it off," he said. "Knock it off."

"Just a Mexican *abrazo*, Horace. Custom of the country. Everyone does it down here."

"I don't care what the custom is. Just keep away from me."

"Horace! Why are you so cold?"

Horace said, "Knock it off, will you?" and walked out. A little later he came back and stood at the end of the bar drinking a beer.

Weston and Al and Richard came over and stood with Lee. "We're with you, Bill," Weston said. "If he lays a finger on you, I'll break a beer bottle over his head."

Lee did not want to push the routine past a joking stage. He said, "Oh, Horace is O.K., I guess. But there's a limit to what I can stand still for. Two years he hands me these curt nods. Two years he walks into Lola's and looks around—'Nothing in here but fags,' he says, and goes out on the street to drink his beer. Like I say, there is a limit."

A llerton came back from his trip to Morelia sullen and irritable. When Lee asked if he had a good trip, Allerton muttered, "Oh, all right," and went in the other room to play chess with Mary. Lee felt a charge of anger pass through his body. "I'll make him pay for this somehow," he thought.

Lee considered buying a half interest in the Ship Ahoy. Allerton existed on credit at the Ship Ahoy and owed four hundred pesos. If Lee were half owner of the joint, Allerton would not be in a position to ignore him. Lee did not actually want retaliation. He felt a desperate need to maintain some special contact with Allerton.

Lee managed to reestablish contact. One afternoon Lee and Allerton went to visit Al Hyman, who was in the hospital with jaundice. On the way home they stopped in the Bottoms Up for a cocktail.

"What about this trip to South America?" Lee said abruptly.

"Well, it's always nice to see places you haven't seen before," said Allerton.

"Can you leave anytime?"

"Anytime."

Next day Lee started collecting the necessary visas and tickets. "Better buy some camping equipment here," he said. "We may have to trek back into the jungle to find the Yage. When we get where the Yage is, we'll dig a hip cat and ask him, 'Where can we score for Yage?'"

"How will you know where to look for the Yage?" said Allerton.

"I aim to find that out in Bogotá. A Colombian scientist who lives in Bogotá isolated Telepathine from Yage. We must find that scientist."

"Suppose he won't talk?"

"They all talk when Boris goes to work on them."

"You Boris?"

"Certainly not. We pick up Boris in Panama. He did excellent work with the Reds in Barcelona and with the Gestapo in Poland. A talented man. All his work has the Boris touch. Light, but persuasive. A mild little fellow with spectacles. Looks like a bookkeeper. I met him in a Turkish bath in Budapest."

A blond Mexican boy went by pushing a cart. "Jesus Christ!" said Lee, his mouth dropping open. "One of them blond-headed Mexicans! 'Taint as if it was being queer, Allerton. After all, they's only Mexicans. Let's have a drink."

They left by bus a few days later, and by the time they reached Panama City, Allerton was already complaining that Lee was too demanding in his desires. Otherwise, they got on very well. Now that Lee could spend days and nights with the object of his attentions, he felt relieved of the gnawing emptiness and fear. And Allerton was a good traveling companion, sensible and calm.

CHAPTER 7

Lee was reading aloud to Allerton a lurid account of the jungle dives in Panama: "'Anything goes in these dens at the end of perilous muddy roads in the jungles that surround Panama City. . . . Snakes, mosquitoes carrying yellow fever and malaria are the least of the hazards one can expect to encounter. Dope peddlers lurk in the lavatory, offering their wares and sometimes darting out of a toilet booth to administer an injection without waiting for consent. Swamps teeming with alligators can swallow an unwary visitor without a trace. . . .'"

"Well," said Allerton, "what are we waiting for?"

After making an arrangement with a cabdriver to take them there and back for twenty dollars, Lee and Allerton entered a tin-roofed shack with a bar along one wall, some tables, and several listless middle-aged B-girls with barely the energy left to hustle and mooch. The only thing lurking in the lavatory was an insolent, demanding attendant. . . . They did buy some very good green from the cabdriver, whose name was Jones.

The hotel was air-conditioned. The eggs at breakfast were greasy and repulsive. Allerton discovered that you could buy paregoric in the drugstores without prescription.

There was a number on the jukebox in one of the interchangeable bars, called "Opio y Anejo"—"Opium and Rum." Chinese, Lee gathered, since it was sung in a yacking falsetto.

Want to pick up on some grass?"

"That will do for a start."

They got in a cab and smoked the tea. It was very good weed. Lee had never smoked better. Lee asked about getting some H and C.

"Sure man, anything. But it costs, see? Twenty dollars a gram."

Lee cashed a fifty-dollar traveler's check in a curio store, buying a wallet and a Panama hat. His senses were numbed with paregoric and rum and weed. They went around to a series of bars and hotels and whorehouses, looking to score for H and C—for Henry and Charlie.

Allerton passed out on the backseat. Weed always made him sleep. Lee sniffed some stuff in the car. He couldn't tell whether it was anywhere or not. The fifty dollars was gone.

Next day Lee said: "In 1873 the pope issued a bull to the effect there would be no more discussion of the Immaculate Conception. I am issuing a similar bull in regard to that fifty dollars."

CHAPTER 8

They flew from Panama to Quito in a tiny plane which had to struggle to climb above an overcast. The steward plugged in oxygen. Lee sniffed the oxygen hose. "It's cut!" he said in disgust.

They drove into Quito in a windy, cold twilight. The hotel looked a hundred years old. The room had a high ceiling with black beams and white plaster walls. They sat on the beds, shivering. Lee was a little junk sick.

They walked around the main square. Lee hit a drugstore: no paregoric without a script. A cold wind from the high mountains blew rubbish through the dirty streets. The people walked by in gloomy silence. Many had blankets wrapped around their faces. A row of hideous old hags, huddled in dirty blankets that looked like old burlap sacks, were ranged along the walls of a church.

"Now, son, I want you to know I am different from other citizens you might run into. Some people will give you the women-are-no-good routine. I'm not like that. You just pick yourself one of these señoritas and take her right back to the hotel with you."

Allerton looked at Lee. "I think I will get laid tonight," he said.

"Sure," Lee said. "Go right ahead. They don't have much pulchritude in this dump, but that hadn't oughta deter you young fellers. Was it Frank Harris said he never saw an ugly woman till he was thirty? It was, as a matter of fact. . . . Let's go back to the hotel and have a drink."

The bar was drafty. Oak chairs with black leather seats. They ordered martinis. At the next table a red-faced American in an expensive brown gabardine suit was talking about some deal involving twenty thousand acres. Across from Lee was an Ecuadorian man, with a long nose and a spot of red on each cheekbone, dressed in a black suit of European cut. He was drinking coffee and eating sweet cakes.

Lee drank several cocktails. He was getting sicker by the minute.

"Why don't you smoke some weed?" Allerton suggested. "That might help."

"Good idea. Let's go up to the room."

Lee smoked a stick of tea on the balcony. "My God, is it cold out on that balcony," he said, coming back into the room.

"'. . . And when twilight falls on the beautiful old colonial city of Quito and those cool breezes steal down from the Andes, walk out in the fresh of the evening and look over the beautiful señoritas who seat themselves, in colorful native costume, along the wall of the sixteenth-century church that overlooks the main square. . . .' They fired the guy wrote that. There *are* limits, even in a travel folder.

"Tibet must be about like this. High and cold and full of ugly looking people and llamas and yaks. Yak milk for breakfast, yak curds for lunch, and for dinner a yak boiled in his own butter, and a fitting punishment for a yak, too, if you ask me.

"You can smell one of them holy men ten miles downwind on a clear day. Sitting there pulling on his old prayer wheel so nasty. Wrapped in dirty old burlap sacks, with bedbugs crawling around where his neck sticks out of the sack. His nose is all rotted away, and he spits betel nut out through the nose holes like a spitting cobra. . . . Give me that wisdom-of-the-East routine.

"So we got like a holy man, and some bitch reporter comes to interview him. He sits there chewing on his betel nut. After a while, he says to one of his acolytes, 'Go down to the Sacred Well and bring me a dipper of paregoric. I'm going to make with the wisdom of the East. And shake the lead outa your loin cloth!' So he drinks the P.G. and goes into a light trance, and makes cosmic contact—we call it going on the nod in the trade. The reporter says, 'Will there be war with Russia, Mahatma? Will Communism destroy the civilized world? Is the soul immortal? Does God exist?'

"The Mahatma opens his eyes and compresses his lips and spits two long red streams of betel nut juice out through his nose holes. It runs down over his mouth, and he licks it back in with a long, coated tongue and says, 'How in the fuck should I know?' The acolyte says, 'You heard the man. Now cut. The Swami wants to be alone with his medications.' Come to think of it, that *is* the wisdom of the East. The Westerner thinks there is some secret he can discover. The East says, 'How the fuck should I know?'"

That night Lee dreamed he was in a penal colony. All around were high, bare mountains. He lived in a boardinghouse that was never warm. He went out for a walk. As he stepped off a street corner onto a dirty cobblestone street, the cold mountain wind hit him. He tightened the belt of his leather jacket and felt the chill of final despair.

Lee woke up and called to Allerton, "Are you awake, Gene?"

"Yes."

"Cold?"

"Yes."

"Can I come over with you?"

"Ahh, well all right."

Lee got in bed with Allerton. He was shaking with cold and junk sickness.

"You're twitching all over," said Allerton. Lee pressed against him, convulsed by the adolescent lust of junk sickness.

"Christ almighty, your hands are cold," said Allerton.

When Allerton was asleep, he rolled over and threw his knee across Lee's body. Lee lay still so Allerton wouldn't wake up and move away.

T he next day Lee was really sick. They wandered around Quito. The more Lee saw of Quito, the more the place brought him down. The town was hilly, the streets narrow. Allerton stepped off the high curb and a car grazed him. "Thank God you're not hurt," Lee said. "I sure would hate to be stuck in this town."

They sat down in a little coffeehouse where some German refugees hung out, talking about visas and extensions and work permits. They got into a conversation with a man at the next table. The man was thin and blond, his head caved in at the temples. Lee could see the blue veins pulsing in the cold, high-mountain sunlight that covered the man's weak, ravaged face and spilled over the scarred oak table onto the worn wooden floor. Lee asked the man if he liked Quito.

The man said, "To be or not to be, that is the question. I have to like it."

They walked out of the coffeehouse and up the street to a small park. The trees were stunted by wind and cold. A few boys were rowing around and around in a small pond. Lee watched them, torn by lust and curiosity. He saw himself desperately rummaging through bodies and rooms and closets in a frenzied search, a recurrent nightmare. At the end of the search was an empty room. He shivered in the cold wind.

Allerton said, "Why don't you ask those Germans in the coffee shop for the name of a doctor?"

"That's a good idea."

The doctor lived in a yellow stucco villa on a quiet side street. He was Jewish, with a smooth red face, and spoke good English. Lee put down a dysentery routine. The doctor asked a few questions. He started to write out a prescription. Lee said, "The prescription that works best is paregoric with bismuth."

The doctor laughed. He gave Lee a long look. Finally he said, "Tell the truth now." He raised a forefinger, smiling. "Are you addicted to opiates? Better you tell me. Otherwise I cannot help you."

Lee said, "Yes."

"Ah ha," said the doctor. He crumpled up the prescription he was writing and dropped it in the wastebasket. He asked Lee how long the addiction had lasted. He shook his head, looking at Lee. "*Ach*," he said, "you are a young person. You must stop this habit. So you lose your life. Better you should suffer now than continue this habit." The doctor gave Lee a long, human look.

"My God," Lee thought, "what you have to put up with in this business." He nodded and said, "Of course, Doctor, and I want to stop. But I have to get some sleep. I am going to the coast tomorrow, to Manta."

The doctor sat back in his chair, smiling. "You must stop this habit." He ran through the routine again. Lee nodded abstractedly. Finally the doctor reached for his prescription pad: three cc's of tincture.

The drugstore gave Lee paregoric instead of tincture. Three cc's of P.G. Less than a teaspoonful. Nothing. Lee bought a bottle of antihistamine tablets and took a handful. They seemed to help a little.

Lee and Allerton took a plane the next day for Manta.

The Hotel Continental in Manta was made of split bamboo and rough boards. Lee found some knotholes in the wall of their room and plugged the holes up with paper. "We don't want to get deported under a cloud," he said to Allerton. "I'm a little junk sick, you know, and that makes me sooo sexy. The neighbors could witness some innaresting sights."

"I wish to register a complaint concerning breach of contract," said Allerton. "You said twice a week."

"So I did. Well, of course the contract is more or less elastic, you might say. But you are right. Twice a week it is, sire. Of course, if you get hot pants between times, don't hesitate to let me know."

"I'll give you a buzz."

The water was just right for Lee, who could not stand cold water. There was no shock when he plunged in. They swam for an hour or so, then sat on the beach looking at the sea. Allerton could sit for hours doing absolutely nothing. He said, "That boat out there has been warming up for the past hour."

Lee said, "I am going into town to dig the local *bodegas* and buy a bottle of cognac."

The town looked old, with limestone streets and dirty saloons crowded with sailors and dockworkers. A shoeshine boy asked Lee if he wanted "nice girl." Lee looked at the boy and thought, "No, and I don't want you either."

He bought a bottle of cognac from a Turkish trader. The store had everything: ship stores, hardware, guns, food, liquor. Lee priced the guns: three hundred dollars for a .30-30 lever-action Winchester carbine that sold for seventy-two dollars in the States. The Turk said duty was high on guns. That was the reason for this price.

Lee walked back along the beach. The houses were all split bamboo on wood frame, the four posts set directly in the ground. The simplest type of house construction: you set four heavy posts deep in the ground and nail the house to the posts. The houses were built about six feet off the ground. The streets were mud. Thousands of vultures roosted on the houses and walked around the streets, pecking at offal. Lee kicked at a vulture, and the bird flapped away with an indignant squawk.

Lee passed a bar, a large building set directly on the ground, and decided to go in for a drink. The split-bamboo walls shook with noise. Two middle-aged wiry little men were doing an obscene mambo routine opposite each other, their leathery faces creased in toothless smiles. The waiter came up and smiled at Lee. He didn't have any front teeth either. Lee sat down on a short wood bench and ordered a cognac.

A boy of sixteen or so came over and sat down with Lee and smiled an open, friendly smile. Lee smiled back and ordered a *refresco* for the boy. He dropped a hand on Lee's thigh and squeezed it in thanks for the drink. The boy had uneven teeth, crowded one over the other, but he was a

young boy. Lee looked at him speculatively; he couldn't figure the score. Was the boy giving him a come-on, or was he
just friendly? He knew that people in the Latin American
countries were not self-conscious about physical contact.
Boys walked around with their arms around each other's
necks. Lee decided to play it cool. He finished his drink,
shook hands with the boy, and walked back to the hotel.

Allerton was still sitting on the porch in his swimming
trunks and a short-sleeved yellow shirt, which flapped
around his thin body in the evening wind. Lee went inside
to the kitchen and ordered ice and water and glasses. He
told Allerton about the Turk, the town, and the boy. "Let's
go dig that bar after dinner," he said.

"And get felt up by those young boys?" said Allerton.
"I should say not."

Lee laughed. He was feeling surprisingly well. The
antihistamine cut his junk sickness to a vague malaise,
something he would not have noticed if he did not know
what it was. He looked out over the bay, red in the setting
sun. Boats of all sizes were anchored in the bay. Lee wanted
to buy a boat and sail up and down the coast. Allerton liked
the idea. Lee could see the boat anchored at twilight. He
was smoking weed with Gene, sitting beside him on a bunk
in the cabin. He had an arm around Gene's shoulders. They
were both wearing swimming trunks. The sea was glassy.
He saw a fish rise in a swirl of water. He lay down with his
head in Allerton's lap. He felt peaceful and happy. He had
never felt that way in his life, except maybe as a young
child. He couldn't remember. The bitter shocks of his
childhood had blacked out memory of happy times.

"While we are in Ecuador we must score for Yage," Lee said. "Think of it: thought control. Take anyone apart and rebuild to your taste. Anything about somebody bugs you, you say, 'Yage! I want that routine took clear out of his mind.' I could think of a few changes I might make in you, doll." He looked at Allerton and licked his lips. "You'd be so much *nicer* after a few alterations. You're nice now, of course, but you do have those irritating little peculiarities. I mean, you won't do exactly what I want you to do all the time."

"Do you think there is anything in it, really?" Allerton asked.

"The Russians seem to think so. I understand Yage is the most efficient confession drug. They have also used peyote. Ever try it?"

"No."

"Horrible stuff. Made me sick like I wanted to die. I got to puke and I can't. Just excruciating spasms of the asparagus, or whatever you call that gadget. Finally the peyote comes up solid like a ball of hair, solid all the way up, clogging my throat. As nasty a sensation as I ever stood still for. The high is interesting but hardly worth the sick stage. Your face swells around the eyes, and the lips swell, and you look and feel like an Indian, or what you figure an Indian feels like. Primitive, you understand. Colors are more intense but somehow flat and two-dimensional. Everything looks like a peyote plant. There is a nightmare undercurrent.

"I had nightmares after using it, one after the other, every time I went back to sleep. In one dream I had rabies and looked in the mirror and my face changed and I began howling. Another dream I had a chlorophyll habit. Me and five other chlorophyll addicts are waiting to score. We turn green and we can't kick the chlorophyll habit. One shot and you are hung for life. We are turning into plants. You know anything about psychiatry? Schizophrenia?"

"Not much."

"In some cases of schizophrenia a phenomenon occurs known as automatic obedience. I say, 'Stick out your tongue,' and you can't keep yourself from obeying. Whatever I say, whatever anyone says, you must do. Get the picture? A pretty picture, isn't it? so long as you are the one giving the orders that are automatically obeyed. Automatic obedience, synthetic schizophrenia, mass-produced to order. That is the Russian dream, and America is not far behind. The bureaucrats of both countries want the same thing: Control. The superego, the controlling agency, gone cancerous and berserk. Incidentally, there is a connection between schizophrenia and telepathy. Schizos are very telepathically sensitive, but as strictly *receivers*. Dig the tie-in?"

"But you wouldn't know Yage if you saw it."

Lee thought a minute. "Much as I dislike the idea, I will have to go back to Quito and talk to a botanist at the Botanical Institute there."

"I'm not going back to Quito for anything," said Allerton.

"I'm not going right away. I need some rest, and I want to kick the Chinaman all the way out. No need for you to go. You stay on the beach. Papa will go and get the info."

CHAPTER 9

From Manta they flew to Guayaquil. The road was flooded, so the only way to get there was by plane or boat.

Guayaquil is built along a river, a city with many parks and squares and statues. The parks are full of tropical trees and shrubs and vines. A tree that fans out like an umbrella, as wide as it is tall, shades the stone benches. The people do a great deal of sitting.

One day Lee got up early and went to the market. The place was crowded. A curiously mixed populace: Negro, Chinese, Indian, European, Arab, characters difficult to classify. Lee saw some beautiful boys of mixed Chinese and Negro stock, slender and graceful with beautiful white teeth.

A hunchback with withered legs was playing crude bamboo panpipes, a mournful Oriental music with the final sadness of high mountains. In deep sadness there is no place for sentimentality. It is as final as the mountains: a fact. There it is. When you realize it, you cannot complain.

People crowded around the musician, listened a few minutes, and walked on. Lee noticed a young man with the skin tight over his small face, looking exactly like a shrunken head. He could not have weighed more than ninety pounds.

The musician coughed from time to time. Once he snarled when someone touched his hump, showing his black, rotten teeth. Lee gave the man a few coins. He walked on, looking at every face he passed, looking into doorways and up at the windows of cheap hotels. An iron bedstead painted light pink, a shirt out to dry . . . scraps of life. Lee snapped at them hungrily, like a predatory fish cut off from his prey by a glass wall. He could not stop ramming his nose against the glass in the nightmare search of his dream. And at the end he was standing in a dusty room in the late afternoon sun, with an old shoe in his hand.

The city, like all Ecuador, produced a curiously baffling impression. Lee felt there was something going on here, some undercurrent of life that was hidden from him. This was the area of the ancient Chimu pottery, Lee's wet-dream country. Here salt shakers and water pitchers were nameless obscenities: two men on all fours engaged in sodomy formed the handle for the top of a kitchen pot.

What happens when there is no limit? What is the fate of The Land Where Anything Goes? Men changing into huge centipedes . . . centipedes besieging the houses . . . a man tied to a couch and a centipede ten feet long rear-ing up over him. Is this literal? Did some hideous meta-morphosis occur? What is the meaning of the centipede symbol?

Lee got on a bus and rode to the end of the line. He took another bus. He rode out to the river and drank a soda and watched some boys swimming in the dirty river. The river looked as if nameless monsters might rise out of the green-brown water. Lee saw a lizard two feet long run up the opposite bank.

He walked back toward town. He passed a group of boys on a corner. One of the boys was so beautiful the image cut Lee's senses like a wire whip. A slight, invol-untary sound of pain escaped from Lee's lips. He turned around, as if looking at the street name. The boy was laugh-ing at some joke, a high-pitched laugh, happy and gay. Lee walked on.

Six or seven boys, aged twelve to fourteen, were playing in a heap of rubbish on the waterfront. One of the boys was urinating against a post and smiling at the other boys. The boys noticed Lee. Now their play was overtly sexual, with an undercurrent of mockery. They looked at Lee and whis-pered and laughed. Lee looked at them openly, a cold, hard stare of naked lust. He felt the tearing ache of limitless desire.

He focused on one boy, the image sharp and clear, as if seen through a telescope with the other boys and the wa-terfront blacked out. The boy vibrated with life like a young animal. A wide grin showed sharp white teeth. Under the torn shirt Lee glimpsed the thin body. He could feel him-self in the body of the boy. Fragmentary memories . . . the smell of cocoa beans drying in the sun, bamboo tenements, the warm dirty river, the swamps and rubbish heaps on the outskirts of the town.

He was with the other boys, sitting on the stone floor of a deserted house. The roof was gone. The stone walls were falling down. Weeds and vines grew over the walls and stretched across the floor. The boys were taking down their torn pants. Lee lifted his thin buttocks to slip down his pants. He could feel the stone floor. He had his pants down to his ankles. His knees were clasped together, and the other boys were trying to pull them apart. He gave in, and they held his knees open. He looked at them and smiled, and slipped his hand down over his stomach. Another boy who was standing up dropped his pants and stood there with his hands on his hips, looking down at his erect organ.

A boy sat down by Lee and reached over between Lee's legs. Lee felt the orgasm blackout in the hot sun. He stretched out and threw his arm over his eyes. Another boy rested his head on Lee's stomach. Lee could feel the warmth of the other's head, itching a little where the hair touched his stomach.

Now he was in a bamboo tenement. An oil lamp lit a woman's body. Lee could feel desire for the woman through the other's body. "I'm not queer," he thought. "I'm disembodied."

Lee walked on, thinking, "What can I do? Take them back to my hotel? They are willing enough. For a few sucres . . ." He felt a killing hate for the stupid, ordinary, disapproving people who kept him from doing what he wanted to do. "Someday I am going to have things just like I want," he said to himself. "And if any moralizing son of a bitch gives me any static, they will fish him out of the river."

Lee's plan involved a river. He lived on the river and ran things to please himself. He grew his own weed and poppies and cocaine, and he had a young native boy for an all-purpose servant. He licked his lips and looked around. The waterfront was crowded and dirty. All kinds of boats were moored in the dirty river. Great masses of water hyacinth floated by. The river was a good half mile across.

Lee walked up to a little park. There was a statue of Bolívar, "The Liberating Fool" as Lee called him, shaking hands with someone else. Both of them looked tired and disgusted and rocking queer, so queer it rocked you. The statue was on a semicircular base of stone. The statue faced the city. On the other side, facing the water, was a stone bench. Lee stood looking at the statue. Then he sat down on the stone bench facing the river. Everyone looked at Lee when he sat down. Lee looked back. He did not have the American reluctance to meet the gaze of a stranger. The others looked away and lit cigarettes and resumed their conversations.

Lee sat there looking at the dirty yellow river. He couldn't see half an inch under the surface. From time to time, small fish jumped ahead of a boat. There were trim, expensive sailing boats from the yacht club, with hollow masts and beautiful lines. There were dugout canoes with outboard motors and cabins of split bamboo. Two old rusty battleships were moored in the middle of the river: the Ecuadorian Navy. Lee sat there a full hour, then got up and walked back to the hotel. The pension where they were staying was a gray wooden building on the main street, with iron balconies.

It was three o'clock. Allerton was still in bed. Lee sat down on the edge of the bed. "It's three o'clock, Gene," he said. "Time to get up."

"What for?"

"You want to spend your life in bed? Come on out and dig the town with me. I saw some beautiful boys on the waterfront. The real uncut boy stuff. Such teeth, such smiles. Young bodies vibrating with life."

"All right. Stop drooling."

"What have they got that I want, Gene? Do you know?"

"No."

"They have maleness, of course. So have I. I want myself the same way I want others. I'm disembodied. I can't use my own body for some reason." Lee put out his hand. Allerton dodged away.

"What's the matter?"

"I thought you were going to run your hand down my ribs."

"I wouldn't do that. Think I'm queer or something?"

"Frankly, yes."

"You do have nice ribs. Show me the broken one. Is that it there?" Lee ran his hand halfway down Allerton's ribs. "Or is it further down?"

"Oh, go away."

"But, Gene . . . I am due, you know."

"Yes, I suppose you are."

"Of course, if you'd rather wait until tonight . . . These tropical nights are so romantic. That way we could take twelve hours or so and do the thing right." Lee ran his hands down over Allerton's stomach. He could see that Allerton was a little excited.

Allerton said, "Maybe it would be better now. You know I like to sleep alone."

"Yes, I know. Too bad. If I had my way, we'd sleep every night all wrapped around each other like hibernating rattlesnakes."

Lee was taking off his clothes. He lay down beside Allerton. "Wouldn't it be boofül if we should juth run together into one gweat big blob," he said in baby talk. "Am I giving you the horrors?"

"Indeed you are."

Allerton surprised Lee by an unusual intensity of response. At the climax he squeezed Lee hard around the ribs. He sighed deeply and closed his eyes.

Lee smoothed Allerton's eyebrows with his thumbs. "Do you mind that?" he asked.

"Not terribly."

"But you do enjoy it sometimes? The whole deal, I mean."

"Oh, yes."

Lee lay on his back with one cheek against Allerton's shoulder, and went to sleep.

The food was terrible, but the room without meals was almost the same as full *pensión*. They tried one lunch. A plate of rice without sauce, without anything. Allerton said, "I am hurt." A tasteless soup with some fibrous material floating in it that looked like soft, white wood. The main course was a nameless meat as impossible to identify as to eat. "I'd like to dig the cook. I wonder what type character could do this sort of thing."

Lee said, "The cook has barricaded himself in the kitchen. He is shoving this slop out through a slot." The food was, as a matter of fact, passed out through a slot in a door from a dark, smoky room where, presumably, it was being prepared.

Lee decided to apply for a passport before leaving Guayaquil. He was changing clothes to visit the embassy, and talking to Allerton. "Wouldn't do to wear high shoes. The consul is probably an elegant pansy. . . . 'My dear, can you believe it? High shoes. I mean real old buttonhooky shoes. I simply couldn't take my eyes off those shoes. Straight from Dickens. I'm afraid I have no idea what he wanted.'

"I hear they are purging the State Department of queers. If they do, they will be operating with a skeleton staff. . . . Ah, here they are." Lee was putting on a pair of low shoes. "Imagine walking in on the consul and asking him right out for money to eat on. He rears back and claps a scented handkerchief over his mouth, as if you had dropped a dead fish on his desk: 'You're broke! Really, I don't know why you come to me with this revolting disclosure. You might show a modicum of consideration. You must realize how distasteful this sort of thing is. Have you no pride?'"

Lee turned to Allerton. "How do I look? Don't want to look too good or he will be trying to get in my pants. Maybe *you'd* better go. That way we'll get our passports by tomorrow."

"Listen to this." Lee was reading from a Guayaquil paper. "It seems that the Peruvian delegates at the antituberculosis congress in Salinas appeared at the meeting carrying huge maps on which were shown the parts of Ecuador appropriated by Peru in the 1939 war. The Ecuadorian doctors might go to the meeting twirling shrunken heads of Peruvian soldiers on their watch chains."

Allerton had found an article about the heroic fight put up by Ecuador's Wolves of the Sea.

"Their what?"

"That's what it says: *Lobos del Mar.* It seems that one officer stuck by his gun, even though the mechanism was no longer operating."

"Sounds simpleminded to me."

They decided to look for a boat in Las Playas. Las Playas was cold and the water was rough and muddy, a dreary middle-class resort.

They decided to go on to Salinas the next day. That night Lee wanted to go to bed with Allerton, but he refused and the next morning Lee said he was sorry he asked so soon after the last time, which was a breach of contract.

Allerton said, "I don't like people who apologize at breakfast."

Lee said, "Really, Gene, aren't you taking an unfair advantage? Like someone was junk sick and I don't use junk. I say, 'Sick? Really, I don't know why you tell me about your disgusting condition. You might at least have the decency to keep it to yourself. I hate sick people. You must realize how distasteful it is to see you sneezing and yawning and retching. Why don't you go someplace where I won't have to look at you? You've no idea how tiresome you are, or how disgusting. Have you no pride?'"

Allerton said, "That isn't fair at all."

"It isn't supposed to be fair. Just a routine for your amusement, containing a modicum of truth. Hurry and finish your breakfast. We'll miss the Salinas bus."

Salinas had the quiet, dignified air of an upper-class resort town. They had come in the off-season. When they went to swim they found out why this was not the season: the Humboldt Current makes the water cold during the summer months. Allerton put his foot in the water and said, "It's nothing but cold," and refused to go in. Lee plunged in and swam for a few minutes. The water was shockingly cold.

Time seemed to speed up in Salinas. Lee would eat lunch and lie on the beach. After a period that seemed like an hour, or at most two hours, he saw the sun low in the sky: six o'clock. Allerton reported the same experience.

Lee went to Quito to get information on the Yage. Allerton stayed in Salinas. Lee was back five days later.

"Yage is also known to the Indians as Ayahuasca. Scientific name is *Banisteria caapi*." Lee spread a map out on the bed. "It grows in high jungle on the Amazon side of the Andes. We will go on to Puyo. That is the end of the road. We should be able to locate someone there who can deal with the Indians and get the Yage."

They spent a night in Guayaquil. Lee got drunk before dinner and slept through a movie. They went back to the hotel to go to bed and get an early start in the morning. Lee poured himself some brandy and sat down on the edge of Allerton's bed. "You look sweet tonight," he said, taking off his glasses. "How about a little kiss? Huh?"

"Oh, go away," said Allerton.

"O.K., kid. If you say so. There's plenty of time." Lee poured some more brandy in his glass and lay down on his own bed.

"You know, Gene," he said, "not only have they got poor people in this jerkwater country. They also got, like, rich people. I saw some on the train going up to Quito. I expect they keep a plane revved up in the backyard. I can see them loading television sets and radios and golf clubs and tennis rackets and shotguns into the plane, and then trying to boot a prize Brahma bull in on top of the other junk, so the windup is the plane won't get off the ground.

"It's a small, unstable, undeveloped country. Economic setup is classically simple and exactly the way I figured it:

all raw materials, lumber, food, labor, rent very cheap. All manufactured goods very high, because of import duty. The duty is supposed to protect Ecuadorian industry. There is no Ecuadorian industry. No production here. The people who can produce won't produce, because they don't want any money tied up here. They want to be ready to pull out right now, with a bundle of cold cash, preferably U.S. dollars. They are unduly alarmed. Rich people are generally frightened. I don't know why. Something to do with a guilt complex, I imagine. *¿Quién sabe?* I have not come to psychoanalyze Caesar but to protect his person. At a price, of course. What they need here is a security department, to keep the underdog under."

"Yes," said Allerton. "We must secure uniformity of opinion."

"Opinion! What are we running here, a debating society? Give me one year and the people won't have any opinions. 'Now just fall in line here, folks, for your nice tasty stew of fish heads and rice and oleomargarine. And over here for your ration of free lush laced with opium.' So if they get out of line, we jerk the junk out of the lush and they're all lying around shitting in their pants, too weak to move. An eating habit is the worst habit you can have. Another angle is malaria. A debilitating affliction, tailor-made to water down the revolutionary spirit."

Lee smiled. "Just imagine some old humanist German doctor. I say, 'Well, Doc, you done a great job here with malaria. Cut the incidence down almost to nothing.'

"'*Ach*, yes. We do our best, is it not? You see this line in the graph? The line shows the decline in this sickness in the past ten years since we commence with our treatment program.'

"'Yeah, Doc. Now, look, I want to see that line go back where it came from.'

"'*Ach*, this you cannot mean.'

"'And another thing. See if you can't import a specially debilitating strain of hookworm.'

"We can always immobilize the mountain people by taking their blankets away, leaving them with the enterprise of a frozen lizard."

The inside wall to Lee's room stopped about three feet from the ceiling to allow for ventilating the next room, which was an inside room with no windows. The occupant of the next room said something in Spanish to the effect Lee should be quiet.

"Ah, shut up," said Lee, leaping to his feet. "I'll nail a blanket over that slot! I'll cut off your fucking air! You only breathe with my permission. You're the occupant of an inside room, a room without windows. So remember your place and shut your poverty-stricken mouth!"

A stream of *chingas* and *cabrones* replied.

"*Hombre*," said Lee. "*¿En dónde está su cultura?*"

"Let's hit the sack," said Allerton. "I'm tired."

CHAPTER 10

They took a riverboat to Babahoyo. Swinging in hammocks, sipping brandy, and watching the jungle slide by. Springs, moss, beautiful clear streams, and trees up to two hundred feet high. Lee and Allerton were silent as the boat powered upriver, penetrating the jungle stillness with its lawn-mower whine.

From Babahoyo they took a bus over the Andes to Ambato, a cold, jolting fourteen-hour ride. They stopped for a snack of chickpeas at a hut at the top of the mountain pass, far above the tree line. A few young native men in gray felt hats ate their chickpeas in sullen resignation. Several guinea pigs were squeaking and scurrying around on the dirt floor of the hut. Their cries reminded Lee of the guinea pig he owned as a child in the Fairmont Hotel in St. Louis, when the family was waiting to move into their new house on Price Road. He remembered the way the pig shrieked, and the stink of its cage.

They passed the snow-covered peak of Chimborazo, cold in the moonlight and the constant wind of the high Andes. The view from the high-mountain pass seemed from another, larger planet than Earth. Lee and Allerton huddled together under a blanket, drinking brandy, the smell of wood smoke in their nostrils. They were both wearing army-surplus jackets zipped up over sweatshirts to keep out the cold and wind. Allerton seemed insubstantial as a phantom; Lee could almost see through him to the empty phantom bus outside.

From Ambato to Puyo, along the edge of a gorge a thousand feet deep. There were waterfalls and forests and streams running down over the roadway, as they descended into the lush green valley. Several times the bus stopped to remove large stones that had slid down onto the road.

Lee was talking on the bus to an old prospector named Morgan, who had been thirty years in the jungle. Lee asked him about Ayahuasca.

"Acts on them like opium," Morgan said. "All my Indians use it. Can't get any work out of them for three days when they get on Ayahuasca."

"I think there may be a market for it," Lee said.

Morgan said, "I can get any amount."

They passed the prefabricated bungalows of Shell Mera. The Shell Company had spent two years and twenty million dollars, found no oil, and pulled out.

They got into Puyo late at night and found a room in a ramshackle hotel near the general store. Lee and Allerton were too exhausted to speak, and they fell asleep at once.

Next day Old Man Morgan went around with Lee, trying to score for Ayahuasca. Allerton was still sleeping. They hit a wall of evasion. One man said he would bring some the following day. Lee knew he would not bring any.

They went to a little saloon run by a mulatto woman. She pretended not to know what Ayahuasca was. Lee asked if Ayahuasca was illegal. "No," said Morgan, "but the people are suspicious of strangers."

They sat there drinking puro mixed with hot water and sugar and cinnamon. Lee said his racket was shrunk-down heads. He wanted to start a head-shrinking plant to put the deal on mass-production basis. "Heads rolling off the assembly line. . . ."

Morgan said, "You can't buy those heads at any price. The government forbids it, you know. The blighters were killing people to sell the heads."

Morgan had an inexhaustible fund of old dirty jokes. He was talking about some local character from Canada.

"How did he get down here?" Lee asked.

Morgan chuckled. "How did we all get down here? Spot of trouble in our own country, right?"

Lee nodded, without saying anything.

Old Man Morgan went back to Shell Mera on the afternoon bus to collect some money owed him. Lee talked to a Dutchman named Sawyer who was farming near Puyo. Sawyer told Lee there was an American botanist living in the jungle, a few hours out of Puyo.

"He is trying to develop some medicine. I forget the name. If he succeeds in concentrating this medicine, he says he will make a fortune. Now he is having a hard time. He has nothing to eat out there."

Lee said, "I am interested in medicinal plants. I may pay him a visit."

"He will be glad to see you. But take along some flour or tea or something. They have nothing out there."

Later Lee said to Allerton, "A botanist! What a break. He is our man. We will go tomorrow."

"We can hardly pretend we just happened by," said Allerton. "How are you going to explain your visit?"

"I will think of something. Best tell him right out I want to score for Yage. I figure maybe there is a buck in it for both of us. According to what I hear, he is flat on his ass. We are lucky to hit him in that condition. If he was in the chips and drinking champagne out of galoshes in the whorehouses of Puyo, he would hardly be interested to sell me a few hundred sucres' worth of Yage. And, Gene, for the love of Christ, when we do overhaul this character, please don't say, 'Doctor Cotter, I presume.'"

The hotel room in Puyo was damp and cold. The houses across the street were blurred by the pouring rain, like a city underwater. Lee was picking up articles off the bed and shoving them into a rubberized sack. A .32 automatic pistol, some cartridges wrapped in oiled silk, a small frying pan, tea and flour packed in cans and sealed with adhesive tape, two quarts of puro.

Allerton said, "This booze is the heaviest item, and the bottle's got like sharp edges. Why don't we leave it here?"

"We'll have to loosen his tongue," Lee said. He picked up the sack and handed Allerton a shiny new machete.

"Let's wait till the rain stops," said Allerton.

"Wait till the rain stops!" Lee collapsed on the bed with loud, simulated laughter. "Haw haw haw! Wait till the rain stops! They got a saying down here, like 'I'll pay you what I owe you when it stops raining in Puyo.' Haw haw."

"We had two clear days when we first got here."

"I know. A latter-day miracle. There's a movement on foot to canonize the local padre. *Vámonos, cabrón.*"

Lee slapped Allerton's shoulder and they walked out in the rain, slipping on the wet, muddy cobblestones of the main street.

The trail was corduroy. The wood of the trail was covered with a film of mud. They cut long canes to keep from slipping, but it was slow walking. High jungle with hardwood forest on both sides of the trail. Everywhere was water, springs and streams and rivers of clear, cold water.

"Good trout water," Lee said.

They stopped at several houses to ask where Cotter's place was. Everyone said they were headed right. How far? Two, three hours. Maybe more. Word seemed to have gone ahead. One man they met on the trail shifted his machete to shake hands and said at once, "You are looking for Cotter? He is in his house now."

"How far?" Lee asked.

The man looked at Lee and Allerton. "It will take you about three hours more."

They walked on and on. It was late afternoon now. They flipped a coin to see who would ask at the next house. Allerton lost.

"He says three more hours," Allerton said.

"We been hearing that for the past six hours."

Allerton wanted to rest. Lee said, "No. If you rest, your legs get stiff. It's the worst thing you can do."

"Who told you that?"

"Old Man Morgan."

"Well, Morgan or no, I am going to rest."

"Don't make it too long. It will be a hell of a note if we get caught short, stumbling over snakes and jaguars in the dark and falling into *quebradas*—that's what they call these deep crevices cut by streams of water. Some of them are sixty feet deep and four feet wide. Just room enough to fall in."

They stopped to rest in a deserted house. The walls were gone, but there was a roof that looked pretty sound. "We could stop here in a pinch," said Allerton, looking around.

"A definite pinch. No blankets."

It was dark when they reached Cotter's place, a small thatched hut in a clearing. Cotter was a small, wiry man in his middle fifties. Lee observed that the reception was a bit cool. Lee brought out the liquor, and they all had a drink.

Cotter's wife, a large strong-looking, red-haired woman, made some tea with cinnamon to cut the kerosene taste of the puro. Lee got drunk on three drinks.

Cotter was asking Lee a lot of questions. "How did you happen to come here? Where are you from? How long have you been in Ecuador? Who told you about me? Are you a tourist or traveling on business?"

Lee was drunk. He began talking in junky lingo, explaining that he was looking for Yage, or Ayahuasca. He understood the Russians and the Americans were experimenting with this drug. Lee said he figured there might be a buck in the deal for both of them. The more Lee talked, the cooler Cotter's manner became. The man was clearly suspicious, but why or of what, Lee could not decide.

Dinner was pretty good, considering the chief ingredient was a sort of fibrous root and bananas. After dinner, Cotter's wife said, "These boys must be tired, Jim."

Cotter led the way with a flashlight that developed power by pressing a lever. A cot about thirty inches wide made of bamboo slats. "I guess you can both make out here," he said. Mrs. Cotter was spreading a blanket on the cot as a mattress, with another blanket as cover. Lee lay down on the cot next to the wall. Allerton lay on the outside, and Cotter adjusted a mosquito net.

"Mosquitoes?" Lee asked.

"No, vampire bats," Cotter said shortly. "Good night."

"Good night."

Lee's muscles ached from the long walk. He was very tired. He put one arm across Allerton's chest and snuggled close to the boy's body. A feeling of deep tenderness flowed out from Lee's body at the warm contact. He snuggled closer and stroked Allerton's shoulder gently. Allerton moved irritably, pushing Lee's arm away.

"Slack off, will you, and go to sleep," said Allerton. He turned on his side, with his back to Lee. Lee drew his arm back. His whole body contracted with shock. Slowly he put his hand under his cheek. He felt a deep hurt, as though he were bleeding inside. Tears ran down over his face.

He was standing in front of the Ship Ahoy. The place looked deserted. He could hear someone crying. He saw his little son, and knelt down and took the child in his arms. The sound of crying came closer, a wave of sadness, and now Lee was crying, his body shaking with sobs.

He held little Willy close against his chest. A group of people were standing there in convict suits. Lee wondered what they were doing there and why he was crying.

When Lee woke up, he still felt the deep sadness of his dream. He stretched a hand out toward Allerton, then pulled it back. He turned around to face the wall.

Next morning Lee felt dry and irritable and empty of feeling. He borrowed Cotter's .22 rifle and set out with Allerton to have a look at the jungle. The jungle seemed empty of life.

"Cotter says the Indians have cleaned most of the game out of the area," said Allerton. "They all have shotguns from the money they made working for Shell."

They walked along a trail. Huge trees, some over a hundred feet high, matted with vines, cut off the sunlight.

"May God grant we kill some living creature," Lee said. "Gene, I hear something squawking over there. I'm going to try and shoot it."

"What is it?"

"How should I know? It's alive, isn't it?"

Lee pushed through the undergrowth beside the trail. He tripped on a vine and fell into a saw-toothed plant. When he tried to get up, a hundred sharp points caught his clothes and stuck into his flesh.

"Gene!" he called. "Help me! I been seized by a man-eating plant." Gene cut him free with the machete.

They did not see a living thing in the jungle.

Cotter was supposedly trying to find a way to extract curare from the arrow poison the Indians used. He told Lee there were yellow crows to be found in the region, and yellow catfish with extremely poisonous spines. His wife had gotten spined, and Cotter had to administer morphine for the intense pain. He was a medical doctor.

Lee was struck by the story of the Monkey Woman: a brother and sister had come down to this part of Ecuador to live the simple, healthful life on roots and berries and nuts and palm hearts. Two years later a search party had found them, hobbling along on improvised crutches, toothless and suffering from half-healed fractures. It seems there was no calcium in the area. Chickens couldn't lay eggs: there was nothing to form the shell. Cows gave milk, but it was watery and translucent, with no calcium in it.

The brother went back to civilization and steaks, but the Monkey Woman was still there. She earned her moniker by watching what monkeys ate: anything a monkey eats, she can eat, anybody can eat. It's a handy thing to know, if you get lost in the jungle. Also handy to bring along some calcium tablets. Even Cotter's wife had lost her teeth "inna thervith." His were long gone.

He had a five-foot viper guarding his house from prowlers after his precious curare notes. He also had two tiny monkeys, cute but ill-tempered and equipped with sharp little teeth, and a two-toed sloth. Sloths live on fruit in trees, swinging along upside down and making a sound like a crying baby. On the ground they are helpless. This one just lay there and thrashed about and hissed. Cotter warned them not to touch it, even on the back of the neck, since it could reach around with its strong, sharp claws and drive them through one's hand, then pull it to its mouth and start biting.

Cotter was evasive when Lee asked about Ayahuasca. He said he was not sure Yage and Ayahuasca were the same plant. Ayahuasca was connected with *brujería*—witchcraft. He himself was a white *brujo*. He had access to *brujo* secrets. Lee had no such access.

"It would take you years to gain their confidence."

Lee said he did not have years to spend on the deal. "Can't you get me some?" he asked.

Cotter looked at him sourly. "I have been out here three years," he said.

Lee tried to come on like a scientist. "I want to investigate the properties of this drug," he said. "I am willing to take some as an experiment."

Cotter said, "Well, I could take you down to Canela and talk to the *brujo*. He will give you some to try if I say so."

"That would be very kind," said Lee.

Cotter did not say any more about going to Canela. He did say a lot about how short they were on supplies and how he had no time to spare from his experiments with a curare substitute. After three days Lee saw he was wasting time, and told Cotter they were leaving. Cotter made no attempt to conceal his relief.

TWO YEARS LATER:
MEXICO CITY RETURN

Every time I hit Panama, the place is exactly one month, two months, six months more nowhere, like the progress of a degenerative illness. A shift from arithmetic to geometric progression seems to have occurred. Something ugly and ignoble and subhuman is cooking in this mongrel town of pimps and whores and recessive genes, this degraded leech on the Canal.

A smog of bum kicks hangs over Panama in the wet heat. Everyone here is telepathic on the paranoid level. I walked around with my camera and saw a wood and corrugated iron shack on a limestone cliff in Old Panama, like a penthouse. I wanted a picture of this excrescence, with the albatrosses and vultures wheeling over it against the hot gray sky. My hands holding the camera were slippery with sweat, and my shirt stuck to my body like a wet condom.

An old hag in the shack saw me taking the picture. They always know when you are taking their picture, especially in Panama. She went into an angry consultation with some other ratty-looking people I could not see clearly. Then she walked to the edge of a perilous balcony and made an ambiguous gesture of hostility. I walked on and shot some boys—young, alive, unconscious—playing baseball. They never glanced in my direction.

Down by the waterfront I saw a dark young Indian on a fishing boat. He knew I wanted to take his picture, and every time I swung the camera into position he would look up with young male sulkiness. I finally caught him leaning against the bow of the boat, idly scratching one shoulder. A long white scar across right shoulder and collarbone. Such languid animal grace. I put away my camera and leaned over the hot concrete wall, looking at him. I was running a finger along the scar, down across his naked copper chest and stomach, every cell aching with deprivation. I pushed away from the wall, muttering "Oh Jesus," and walked away, looking around for something to photograph. Many so-called primitives are afraid of cameras. They think it can capture their soul and take it away. There is in fact something obscene and sinister about photography, a desire to imprison, to incorporate, a sexual intensity of pursuit.

A Negro with a felt hat was leaning on the porch rail of a wooden house built on a dirty limestone foundation. I was across the street under a movie marquee. Every time I prepared my camera he would lift his hat and look at me, muttering insane imprecations. I finally snapped him from behind a pillar. On a balcony over this character a shirtless young man was washing. Negro and Near Eastern blood, rounded face, café-au-lait mulatto skin, smooth body of undifferentiated flesh with not a muscle showing. He looked up from his washing like an animal scenting danger. I caught him when the five o'clock whistle blew. Old photographer trick: wait for distraction.

I went into Chico's Bar for a rum Coke. I never liked this place, nor any other bar in Panama, but it used to be endurable and had some good numbers on the jukebox. Now nothing but this awful Oklahoma honky-tonk music, like the bellowing of an anxious cow: "Drivin' Nails in My Coffin," "It Wasn't God Who Made Honky Tonk Angels," "Your Cheatin' Heart."

The servicemen in the joint all had that light-concussion Canal Zone look: cow-like and blunted, as if they had undergone special G.I. processing and were immunized against contact on the intuition level, telepathic sender and receiver excised. You ask them a question, they answer without friendliness or hostility. No warmth, no contact. Conversation is impossible. They just have nothing to say. They sit around buying drinks for the B-girls and make lifeless passes, which the girls brush off like flies, and play that whining music on the jukebox. One young man with a pimply adenoidal face kept trying to touch a girl's breast. She would brush his hand away, then it would creep back as if endowed with autonomous insect life.

A B-girl sat next to me, and I bought her one drink. She ordered good Scotch, yet. "Panama, how I hate your cheatin' guts," I thought. She had a shallow bird brain and perfect stateside English, like a recording. Stupid people can learn a language quick and easy because there is nothing going on in there to keep it out.

She wanted another drink. I said, "No."

She said, "Why are you so mean?"

I said, "Look, if I run out of money, who is going to buy my drinks? Will you?"

She looked surprised, and said slowly, "Yes. You are right. Excuse me."

I walked down the main drag. A pimp seized my arm. "I gotta fourteen-year-old girl, Jack. Puerto Rican. How's about it?"

"She's middle-aged already," I told him. "I want a six-year-old virgin and none of that sealed-while-you-wait shit. Don't try palming your fourteen-year-old bats off on me." I left him there with his mouth open.

I went into a store to price Panama hats. The young man behind the counter started singing: "Making friends, making money."

"This spic bastard is strictly on the chisel," I decided.

He showed me some two-dollar hats. "Fifteen dollar," he said.

"Your prices are way out of line," I told him, and turned and walked out.

He followed me onto the street. "Just a minute, Mister." I walked on.

Flew up to Tapachula just over the Mexican border. Met an old tourist from Texas in the airport—we had arrived on the same plane—and took a taxi with him and checked into the same hotel. I felt better in Mexico. Went into a cantina and ordered rum. A beggar came through with a withered hand. His hand looked something like Allerton's, so I gave him twenty centavos.

That night I had a recurrent dream: I was back in Mexico City, talking to Art Gonzalez, a former roommate of Allerton's. I asked him where Allerton was, and he said, "In Agua Diente." This was somewhere south of Mexico City, and I was inquiring about a bus connection. I have dreamed many times I was back in Mexico City, talking to Art or Allerton's best friend, Johnny White, and asking where he was. Dream about Allerton continually. Usually we are on good terms, but sometimes he is inexplicably hostile, and when I ask why, what is the matter, his answer is muffled. I never find out why.

Flew up to Mexico City. I was a little nervous going through the airport that some cop or immigration inspector might spot me. I decided to stick close to my tourist. I had packed my hat, and when I got off the plane I took off my glasses. I slung my camera over my shoulder.

"Let's take a cab into town. Split the fare. Cheaper that way," I said to the tourist. We walked through the airport like father and son. "Yes," I was saying, "that old boy in Guatemala wanted to charge me two dollars from the Palace Hotel out to the airport. I told him *uno*." I held up one finger. No one looked at us. Two tourists.

We got into a taxi. The driver said twelve pesos for both to the center of town.

"Wait a minute," the tourist said in English. "No meter. Where your meter? You got to have a meter."

The driver asked me to explain they were authorized to carry airline passengers to town without a meter.

"No!" the tourist shouted. "I not tourist. I live in Mexico City. *¿Sabe* Hotel Colmena? I live in Hotel Colmena. Take me to town but I pay what is on meter. I call police. *Policía.* You're required by law to have a meter."

"Oh God," I thought. "That's all I need, this old jerk should call the law." I could see cops accumulating around the cab, not knowing what to do and calling other cops. The tourist got out of the cab with his suitcase. He was taking down the number.

"I call *policía* plenty quick," he said.

I said, "Well, I think I'll take this cab anyway. Won't get into town much cheaper. . . . *Vámonos,*" I said to the driver.

I checked into an eight-peso hotel near Sears, and walked over to Lola's, my stomach cold with excitement. "Easy now. Cool. Cool." The bar was in a different place, redecorated, with new furniture. But there was Pepe behind the bar, with his gold tooth and his moustache.

"*¿Cómo está?*" he said. We shook hands. He asked where I had been, and I told him South America. I sat down with a Delaware Punch. The place was empty, but someone I knew was sure to come in sooner or later.

The Major walked in. A retired army man, gray-haired, vigorous, stocky. I ran through the list crisply with the Major:

"Johnny White, Russ Morton, Pete Crowly, Ike Scranton?"

"Los Angeles, Alaska, Idaho, don't know, still around.
He's always around."

"And oh, uh, whatever happened to Allerton?"

"Allerton? Don't believe I know him."

"See you."

"Right, Lee. Take it easy."

I walked over to Sears and looked through the magazines. In one called *Balls: For Real Men*, I was looking at
a photo of a Negro hanging from a tree: "I Saw Them
Swing Sonny Goons." A hand fell on my shoulder. I turned,
and there was Gale, another retired army man. He had
the subdued air of the reformed drunk. I ran through the
list.

"Most everybody is gone," he said. "I never see those
guys anyway, never hang around Lola's anymore."

I asked about Allerton.

"Allerton?"

"Tall skinny kid. Friend of Johnny White and Art
Gonzalez."

"He's gone too."

"How long ago?" No need to play it cool and casual
with Gale. He wouldn't notice anything.

"I saw him about a month ago on the other side of the
street." A wave of pain and desolation hit me like a main-
line shot settling in the lungs and around the heart.

"See you."

"See you."

I put the magazine away slowly and walked outside and
leaned against a post. "He must have gotten my letters.
Why didn't he answer? Why?"

I walked back to Lola's, the pain inside sharp and definite as a physical wound. Burns was sitting at a table, drinking a beer with his maimed hand.

"Hardly anybody around. Johnny White and Tex and Crosswheel are in Los Angeles."

I was looking at his hand.

"Did you hear about Allerton?" he asked.

I said, "No."

"He went down to South America or some place. With an army colonel. Allerton went along as guide."

"So? How long has he been gone?"

"About six months."

"Must have been right after I left."

"Yeah. Just about then."

I could feel the pain ease up a bit. I got Art Gonzalez's address from Burns and went over to see him. He was drinking a beer in a shop across from his hotel and called me over. Yes, Allerton left about five months ago and went along as guide to a colonel and his wife.

"They were going to sell the car in Guatemala. A '48 Cadillac. I felt there was something not quite right about the deal. But Allerton never told me anything definite. You know how he is." Art seemed surprised I had not heard from Allerton. "Nobody has heard anything from him since he left. It worries me."

I wondered what he could be doing, and where. Guatemala is expensive, San Salvador expensive and jerkwater. Costa Rica? I regretted not having stopped off in San José on the way up.

"He said something about joining you down there."

Evidently, he had no beef. I figured he was in some sort of jam and was afraid his mail might be opened at his home address.

Gonzalez and I went through the where-is-so-and-so routine. Mexico City is a terminal of space-time travel, a waiting room where you grab a quick drink while you wait for your train. That is why I can stand to be in Mexico City or New York. You are not stuck; by the fact of being there at all, you are traveling. But in Panama, crossroads of the world, you are exactly so much aging tissue. You have to make arrangements with Pan Am or the Dutch Line for removal of your body. Otherwise, it would stay there and rot in the muggy heat, under a galvanized iron roof.

Dream that night: I was in Peru-Mexico-N.Y., the City, eating in a restaurant with booths. Restaurant opened onto the backyards and red brick houses of St. Louis 1918. I was wondering where Allerton was. A beggar came to the table and held up a withered hand. Then another beggar selling *Colombian* lottery tickets. Someone pointed out this was not Colombia. The beggar looked hurt and puzzled. He never thought of that. Allerton has the same puzzled and slightly hurt look when I point out that we are not using the same currency.

That night I dreamed I finally found Allerton, hiding out someplace. He seemed surprised to see me after all this time. In the dream I was a finder of missing persons.

"Mr. Allerton, I represent the Friendly Finance Company. Haven't you forgotten something, Gene? You're supposed to come and see us every third Tuesday. We've been lonely for you in the office. We don't like to say 'Pay up or else.' It's not a friendly thing to say. I wonder if you ever read the contract *all the way through*? I have particular reference to Clause 6(x), which can only be deciphered with an electron microscope and a virus filter. I wonder if you know just what '*or else*' means, Gene?

"Aw, I know how it is with you young kids. You get chasing after some floozie and forget all about Friendly Finance, don't you? But Friendly Finance doesn't forget you. Like the song say, 'No hiding place down there.' Not when the old Skip Tracer goes out on a job."

The Skip Tracer's face goes blank and dreamy. His mouth falls open, showing teeth hard and yellow as old ivory. Slowly his body slides down in the leather armchair until the back of the chair pushes his hat down over his eyes. The eyes gleam in the hat's shade, catching points of light like an opal. He begins humming "Johnny's So Long at the Fair" over and over. The humming stops abruptly, in the middle of a phrase.

The Skip Tracer is talking in a voice languid and intermittent, like music down a windy street. "You meet all kinds on this job, kid. Every now and then some popcorn citizen walks in the office and tries to pay Friendly Finance with *this* shit."

He lets one arm swing out, palm up, over the side of the chair. Slowly he opens a thin brown hand, with purple-blue fingertips, to reveal a roll of yellow thousand-dollar bills. The hand turns over, palm down, and falls back against the chair. His eyes close.

Suddenly his head drops to one side and his tongue falls out. The bills drop from his hand, one after the other, and lie there crumpled on the red tile floor. A gust of warm spring wind blows dirty pink curtains into the room. The bills rustle across the room and settle at Allerton's feet.

Imperceptibly the Skip Tracer straightens up, and a slit of light goes on behind each eye.

"Keep that in case you're caught short, kid," he says. "You know how it is in these spic hotels. You gotta carry your own paper."

The Skip Tracer leans forward, his elbows on his knees. Suddenly he is standing up, as if tilted out of the chair, and in the same upward movement he pushes the hat back from his eyes with one finger. He walks to the door and turns, with his right hand on the knob. He polishes the nails of his left hand on the lapel of his worn glen plaid suit. The suit gives out an odor of mold when he moves. There is mildew under the lapels and in the trouser cuffs. He looks at his nails.

"Oh, uh . . . about your, uh . . . account. I'll be around soon. That is, within the next few . . ." The Skip Tracer's voice is muffled.

"We'll come to *some* kind of an agreement." Now the voice is loud and clear. The door opens and wind blows through the room. The door closes and the curtains settle back, one curtain trailing inside the window as if someone had taken it off and tossed it there.

William S. Burroughs' Introduction
to the 1985 Edition

W hen I lived in Mexico City at the end of the 1940s, it was a city of one million people, with clear sparkling air and the sky that special shade of blue that goes so well with circling vultures, blood, and sand—the raw, menacing, pitiless Mexican blue. I liked Mexico City from the first day of my first visit there. In 1949 it was a cheap place to live, with a large foreign colony, fabulous whorehouses and restaurants, cockfights and bullfights, and every conceivable diversion. A single man could live well there for two dollars a day. My New Orleans case for heroin and marijuana possession looked so unpromising that I decided not to show up for the court date, and I rented an apartment in a quiet, middle-class neighborhood of Mexico City.

I knew that under the statute of limitations I could not return to the United States for five years, so I applied for Mexican citizenship and enrolled in some courses in Mayan and Mexican archaeology at Mexico City College. The G.I. Bill paid for my books and tuition, and a seventy-five-dollar-per-month living allowance. I thought I might go into farming or perhaps open a bar on the American border.

The city appealed to me. The slum areas compared favorably with anything in Asia for sheer filth and poverty. People would shit all over the street, then lie down and sleep in it with the flies crawling in and out of their mouths. Entrepreneurs, not infrequently lepers, built fires on street corners and cooked up hideous, stinking, nameless messes of food, which they dispensed to passers-by. Drunks slept right on the sidewalks of the main drag, and no cops bothered them. It seemed to me that everyone in Mexico had mastered the art of minding his own business. If a man wanted to wear a monocle or carry a cane, he did not hesitate to do it, and no one gave him a second glance. Boys and young men walked down the street arm in arm and no one paid them any mind. It wasn't that people didn't care what others thought; it simply would not occur to a Mexican to expect criticism from a stranger, nor to criticize the behavior of others.

Mexico was basically an Oriental culture that reflected two thousand years of disease and poverty and degradation and stupidity and slavery and brutality and psychic and physical terrorism. It was sinister and gloomy and chaotic, with the special chaos of a dream. No Mexican really knew any other Mexican, and when a Mexican killed someone (which happened often), it was usually his best friend. Anyone who felt like it carried a gun, and I read of several occasions where drunken cops, shooting at the habitués of a bar, were themselves shot by armed civilians. As authority figures, Mexican cops ranked with streetcar conductors.

All officials were corruptible, income tax was very low, and medical treatment was extremely reasonable, because the doctors advertised and cut their prices. You could get a clap cured for $2.40, or buy the penicillin and shoot it yourself. There were no regulations curtailing self-medication, and needles and syringes could be bought anywhere. This was in the time of Alemán, when the *mordida* was king, and a pyramid of bribes reached from the cop on the beat up to the *presidente*. Mexico City was also the murder capital of the world, with the highest per capita homicide rate. I remember newspaper stories every day, like these:

A *campesino* is in from the country, waiting for a bus: linen pants, sandals made from a tire, a wide sombrero, a machete at his belt. Another man is also waiting, dressed in a suit, looking at his wristwatch, muttering angrily. The *campesino* whips out his machete and cuts the man's head clean off. He later told police: "He was giving me looks *muy feo* and finally I could not contain myself." Obviously the man was annoyed because the bus was late, and was looking down the road for the bus, when the *campesino* misinterpreted his action, and the next thing a head rolls in the gutter, grimacing horribly and showing gold teeth.

Two *campesinos* are sitting disconsolate by the roadside. They have no money for breakfast. But look: a boy leading several goats. One *campesino* picks up a rock and bashes the boy's brains out. They take the goats to the nearest village and sell them. They are eating breakfast when they are apprehended by the police.

A man lives in a little house. A stranger asks him how to find the road for Ayahuasca. "Ah, this way, señor." He is leading the man around and around: "The road is right here." Suddenly he realizes he hasn't any idea where the road is, and why should he be bothered? So he picks up a rock and kills his tormentor.

Campesinos took their toll with rock and machete. More murderous were the politicians and off-duty cops, each with his .45 automatic. One learned to hit the deck. Here is another actual story: A gun-toting *político* hears his girl is cheating, meeting someone in this cocktail lounge. Some American kid just happens in and sits next to her, when the macho bursts in: "*¡CHINGAO!*" Hauls out his .45 and blasts the kid right off his bar stool. They drag the body outside and down the street a ways. When the cops arrive, the bartender shrugs and mops his bloody bar, and says only: "*¡Malos, esos muchachos!*" ("Those bad boys!")

Every country has its own special Shits, like the Southern lawman counting his nigger notches, and the sneering Mexican macho is certainly up there when it comes to sheer ugliness. And many of the Mexican middle class are about as awful as any bourgeoisie in the world. I remember that in Mexico the narcotic scripts were bright yellow, like a thousand-dollar bill, or a dishonorable discharge from the army. One time Old Dave and I tried to fill such a script, which he had obtained quite legitimately from the Mexican government. The first pharmacist we hit jerked back snarling from such a sight: "*¡No préstamos servicio a los viciosos!*" ("We do not serve dope fiends!")

From one *farmacía* to another we walked, getting sicker with every step. "No, señor. . . ." We must have walked for miles.

"Never been in this neighborhood before."

"Well, let's try one more."

Finally we entered a tiny hole-in-the-wall *farmacía*. I pulled out the *receta*, and a gray-haired lady smiled at me. The pharmacist looked at the script and said, "Two minutes, señor."

We sat down to wait. There were geraniums in the window. A small boy brought me a glass of water, and a cat rubbed against my leg. After a while the pharmacist returned with our morphine.

"*Gracias*, señor."

Outside, the neighborhood now seemed enchanted: Little *farmacías* in a market, crates and stalls outside, a *pulquería* on the corner. Kiosks selling fried grasshoppers and peppermint candy black with flies. Boys in from the country in spotless white linen and rope sandals, with faces of burnished copper and fierce innocent black eyes, like exotic animals, of a dazzling sexless beauty. Here is a boy with sharp features and black skin, smelling of vanilla, a gardenia behind his ear. Yes, you found a Johnson, but you waded through Shitville to find him. You always do. Just when you think the earth is exclusively populated by Shits, you meet a Johnson.

One day there was a knock on my door at eight in the morning. I went to the door in my pyjamas, and there was an inspector from immigration.

"Get your clothes on. You're under arrest."

It seemed the woman next door had turned in a long report on my drunk and disorderly behavior, and also there was something wrong with my papers, and where was the Mexican wife I was supposed to have? The immigration officers were all set to throw me in jail to await deportation as an undesirable alien. Of course, everything could be straightened out with some money, but my interviewer was the head of the deporting department and he wouldn't go for peanuts. I finally had to get up off of two hundred dollars. As I walked home from the immigration office, I imagined what I might have to pay if I had really had an investment in Mexico City.

I thought of the constant problems the three American owners of the Ship Ahoy encountered. The cops came in all the time for a *mordida*, and then came the sanitary inspectors, then more cops trying to get something on the joint so they could take a real bite. They took the waiter downtown and beat the shit out of him. They wanted to know where was Kelly's body stashed? How many women been raped in the joint? Who brought in the weed? And so on. Kelly was an American hipster who had been shot in the Ship Ahoy six months before, had recovered, and was now in the U.S. Army. No woman was ever raped there, and no one ever smoked weed there. By now I had entirely abandoned my plans to open a bar in Mexico.

An addict has little regard for his image. He wears the dirtiest, shabbiest clothes and feels no need to call attention to himself. During my period of addiction in Tangiers, I was known as El Hombre Invisible, The Invisible Man. This disintegration of self-image often results in an indiscriminate image hunger. Billie Holiday said she knew she was off junk when she stopped watching T.V. In my first novel, *Junky*, the protagonist, "Lee," comes across as integrated and self-contained, sure of himself and where he is going. In *Queer* he is disintegrated, desperately in need of contact, completely unsure of himself and of his purpose.

The difference of course is simple: Lee on junk is covered, protected, and also severely limited. Not only does junk short-circuit the sex drive, it also blunts emotional reactions to the vanishing point, depending on the dosage. Looking back over the action of *Queer*, that hallucinated month of acute withdrawal takes on a hellish glow of menace and evil drifting out of neon-lit cocktail bars, the ugly violence, the .45 always just under the surface. On junk I was insulated, didn't drink, didn't go out much, just shot up and waited for the next shot.

When the cover is removed, everything that has been held in check by junk spills out. The withdrawing addict is subject to the emotional excesses of a child or an adolescent, regardless of his actual age. And the sex drive returns in full force. Men of sixty experience wet dreams and spontaneous orgasms (an extremely unpleasant experience, *agaçant* as the French say, putting the teeth on edge). Unless the reader keeps this in mind, the metamorphosis of Lee's character will appear as inexplicable or psychotic. Also bear in mind that the withdrawal syndrome is self-limiting, lasting no more than a month. And Lee has a phase of excessive drinking, which exacerbates all the worst and most dangerous aspects of the withdrawal sickness: reckless, unseemly, outrageous, maudlin—in a word, appalling— behavior.

After withdrawal, the organism readjusts and stabilizes at a pre-junk level. In the narrative, this stabilization is finally reached during the South American trip. No junk is available, nor any other drug, after the paregoric of Panama. Lee's drinking has dwindled to several good stiff ones at sundown. Not so different from the Lee of the later *Yage Letters*, except for the phantom presence of Allerton.

So I had written *Junky*, and the motivation for that was comparatively simple: to put down in the most accurate and simple terms my experiences as an addict. I was hoping for publication, money, recognition. Kerouac had published *The Town and the City* at the time I started writing *Junky*. I remember writing in a letter to him, when his book was published, that money and fame were now assured. As you can see, I knew nothing about the writing business at the time.

My motivations to write *Queer* were more complex, and are not clear to me at the present time. Why should I wish to chronicle so carefully these extremely painful and unpleasant and lacerating memories? While it was I who wrote *Junky*, I feel that I was being written in *Queer*. I was also taking pains to ensure further writing, so as to set the record straight: writing as inoculation. As soon as something is written, it loses the power of surprise, just as a virus loses its advantage when a weakened virus has created alerted antibodies. So I achieved some immunity from further perilous ventures along these lines by writing my experience down.

At the beginning of the *Queer* manuscript fragment,

having returned from the insulation of junk to the land of the living like a frantic, inept Lazarus, Lee seems determined to score, in the sexual sense of the word. There is something curiously systematic and unsexual about his quest for a suitable sex object, crossing one prospect after another off a list which seems compiled with ultimate failure in mind. On some very deep level he does not want to succeed, but will go to any length to avoid the realization that he is not really looking for sex contact.

But Allerton was definitely *some* sort of contact. And what was the contact that Lee was looking for? Seen from here, a very confused concept that had nothing to do with Allerton as a character. While the addict is indifferent to the impression he creates in others, during withdrawal he may feel the compulsive need for an audience, and this is clearly what Lee seeks in Allerton: an audience, the acknowledgment of his performance, which of course is a mask, to cover a shocking disintegration. So he invents a frantic attention-getting format which he calls the Routine: shocking, funny, riveting. "It is an ancient Mariner, / And he stoppeth one of three. . . ."

The performance takes the form of routines: fantasies about Chess Players, the Texas Oil Man, Corn Hole Gus's Used-Slave Lot. In *Queer*, Lee addresses these routines to an actual audience. Later, as he develops as a writer, the audience becomes internalized. But the same mechanism that produced A.J. and Doctor Benway, the same creative impulse, is dedicated to Allerton, who is forced into the role of approving muse, in which he feels understandably uncomfortable.

What Lee is looking for is contact or recognition, like a photon emerging from the haze of insubstantiality to leave an indelible recording in Allerton's consciousness. Failing to find an adequate observer, he is threatened by painful dispersal, like an unobserved photon. Lee does not know that he is already committed to writing, since this is the only way he has of making an indelible record, whether Allerton is inclined to observe or not. Lee is being inexorably pressed into the world of fiction. He has already made the choice between his life and his work.

The manuscript trails off in Puyo, End of the Road town. . . . The search for Yage has failed. The mysterious Doctor Cotter wants only to be rid of his unwelcome guests. He suspects them to be agents of his treacherous partner Gill, intent on stealing his genius work of isolating curare from the composite arrow poison. I heard later that the chemical companies decided simply to buy up the arrow poison in quantity and extract curare in their American laboratories. The drug was soon synthesized and is now a standard substance found in many muscle-relaxing preparations. So it would seem that Cotter really had nothing to lose: his efforts were already superseded.

Dead end. And Puyo can serve as a model for the Place of Dead Roads: a dead, meaningless conglomerate of tin-roofed houses under a continual downpour of rain. Shell has pulled out, leaving prefabricated bungalows and rusting machinery behind. And Lee has reached the end of his line, an end implicit in the beginning. He is left with the impact of unbridgeable distances, the defeat and weariness of a long, painful journey made for nothing, wrong turn-ings, the track lost, a bus waiting in the rain . . . back to Ambato, Quito, Panama, Mexico City.

When I started to write this companion text to *Queer*, I was paralyzed with a heavy reluctance, a writer's block like a straitjacket: "I glance at the manuscript of *Queer* and feel I simply can't read it. My past was a poisoned river from which one was fortunate to escape, and by which one feels immediately threatened, years after the events recorded— painful to an extent I find it difficult to read, let alone to write about. Every word and gesture sets the teeth on edge." The reason for this reluctance becomes clearer as I force myself to look: the book is motivated and formed by an event which is never mentioned, in fact is carefully avoided: the accidental shooting death of my wife, Joan, in September 1951.

While I was writing *The Place of Dead Roads*, I felt in spiritual contact with the late English writer Denton Welch, and modeled the novel's hero, Kim Carsons, di-rectly on him. Whole sections came to me as if dictated, like table tapping. I have written about the fateful morning of Denton's accident, which left him an invalid for the re-mainder of his short life. If he had stayed a little longer here, not so long there, he would have missed his appoint-ment with the female motorist who hit his bicycle from behind for no apparent reason. At one point Denton had stopped to have coffee, and looking at the brass hinges on the café's window shutters, some of them broken, he was hit by a feeling of universal desolation and loss. So every event of that morning is charged with special significance, as if it were underlined. This portentous second sight permeates Welch's writing: a scone, a cup of tea, an inkwell purchased for a few shillings become charged with a special and often sinister significance.

I get exactly the same feeling to an almost unbearable degree as I read the manuscript of *Queer*. The event toward which Lee feels himself inexorably driven is the death of his wife by his own hand, the knowledge of possession, a dead hand waiting to slip over his like a glove. So a smog of menace and evil rises from the pages, an evil that Lee, knowing and yet not knowing, tries to escape with frantic flights of fantasy: his routines, which set one's teeth on edge because of the ugly menace just behind or to one side of them, a presence palpable as a haze.

Brion Gysin said to me in Paris: "For ugly spirit shot Joan because . . ." A bit of mediumistic message that was not completed—or was it? It doesn't need to be completed, if you read it: "ugly spirit shot Joan *to be cause*"; that is, to maintain a hateful parasitic occupation. My concept of possession is closer to the medieval model than to modern psychological explanations, with their dogmatic insistence that such manifestations must come from within and never, never, never from without. (As if there were some clear-cut difference between inner and outer.) I mean a definite possessing entity. And indeed, the psychological concept might well have been devised by the possessing entities, since nothing is more dangerous to a possessor than being seen as a separate, invading creature by the host it has invaded.

And for this reason the possessor shows itself only when absolutely necessary.

In 1939 I became interested in Egyptian hieroglyphics and went out to see someone in the Department of Egyptology at the University of Chicago. And something was screaming in my ear: "YOU DON'T BELONG HERE!" Yes, the hieroglyphics provided one key to the mechanism of possession. Like a virus, the possessing entity must find a port of entry.

This occasion was my first clear indication of something in my being that was not me and not under my control. I remember a dream from this period: I worked as an exterminator in Chicago, in the late 1930s, and lived in a rooming house on the Near North Side. In the dream I am floating up near the ceiling with a feeling of utter death and despair, and looking down I see my body walking out the door with deadly purpose.

One wonders if Yage could have saved the day by a blinding revelation. I remember a cut-up I made in Paris years later: "Raw peeled winds of hate and mischance blew the shot." And for years I thought this referred to blowing a shot of junk, when the junk squirts out the side of the syringe or dropper owing to an obstruction. Brion Gysin pointed out the actual meaning: the shot that killed Joan.

I had bought a Scout knife in Quito. It had a metal handle and a curious tarnished old look, like something from a turn-of-the-century junk shop. I can see it in a tray of old knives and rings, with the silver plate flaking off. It was about three o'clock in the afternoon, a few days after I came back to Mexico City, and I decided to have the knife sharpened. The knife sharpener had a little whistle and a fixed route, and as I walked down the street toward his cart a feeling of loss and sadness that had weighed on me all day so I could hardly breathe intensified to such an extent that I found tears streaming down my face.

"What on earth is wrong?" I wondered.

This heavy depression and a feeling of doom occurs again and again in the text. Lee usually attributes it to his failures with Allerton: "A heavy drag slowed movement and thought. Lee's face was rigid, his voice toneless." Allerton has just refused a dinner invitation and left abruptly: "Lee stared at the table, his thoughts slow, as if he were very cold." (Reading this *I am* cold and depressed.)

Here is a precognitive dream from Cotter's shack in Ecuador: "He was standing in front of the Ship Ahoy. The place looked deserted. He could hear someone crying. He saw his little son, and knelt down and took the child in his arms. The sound of crying came closer, a wave of sadness. . . . He held little Willy close against his chest. A group of people were standing there in convict suits. Lee wondered what they were doing there and why he was crying."

I have constrained myself to remember the day of Joan's death, the overwhelming feeling of doom and loss . . . walking down the street I suddenly found tears streaming down my face. "What is wrong with me?" The small Scout knife with a metal handle, the plating peeling off, a smell of old coins, the knife sharpener's whistle. Whatever happened to this knife I never reclaimed?

I am forced to the appalling conclusion that I would

never have become a writer but for Joan's death, and to a realization of the extent to which this event has motivated and formulated my writing. I live with the constant threat of possession, and a constant need to escape from possession, from Control. So the death of Joan brought me in contact with the invader, the Ugly Spirit, and maneuvered me into a lifelong struggle, in which I have had no choice except to write my way out.

I have constrained myself to escape death. Denton Welch is almost my face. Smell of old coins. Whatever happened to this knife called Allerton, back to the appalling Margaras Inc. The realization is basic formulated doing? The day of Joan's doom and loss. Found tears streaming down from Allerton peeling off the same person as a Western shootist. What are you rewriting? A lifelong preoccupation with Control and Virus. Having gained access the virus uses the host's energy, blood, flesh and bones to make copies of itself. Model of dogmatic insistence never never from without was screaming in my ear, "YOU DON'T BELONG HERE!"

A straitjacket notation carefully paralyzed with heavy reluctance. To escape their prewritten lines years after the events recorded. A writer's block avoided Joan's death. Denton Welch is Kim Carsons' voice through a cloud underlined broken table tapping.

William S. Burroughs
February 1985

Key to Manuscripts

First Q ms.

Fifty-nine-page first-draft typescript of "Queer," mailed to Allen Ginsberg mid-May 1952, plus the twenty-five-page "South American section" mailed in June 1953. The most complete copy is in the William S. Burroughs Papers 1951–1972 at the Henry W. and Albert A. Berg Collection of English and American Literature, New York Public Library, with some carbons and variants also in the Allen Ginsberg Papers at Stanford University (Correspondence Series 1, Box 2, Folder 42).

Second Q ms.

Revised retype of the fifty-nine-page draft, mailed to Ginsberg in late May 1952, one page of which is in the Allen Ginsberg Collection at Columbia University, New York, and two pages of which are in the Ginsberg Papers at Stanford University (as above). The Columbia page, numbered 44 (from "that night. He did not buy a ticket" to "cautious, aging, frightened flesh"), corresponds to pages 52–55 here, but without the section inserted in 1985; see note on page 53, below. The two Stanford pages, numbered 24 and 25 (from "table. Lee felt his stomach knot" to "made horrible screeching noise when the"), correspond to pages 17–18 here.

THIRD Q MS.

Complete retyped manuscript, made by Alene Lee ca. November 1953, five pages of which are in the Ginsberg Papers at Stanford University (as above). This sequence formed the original opening of the manuscript (from "One morning in April" to "He said, smiling at the wait[er.]"), the first half of which was cut in 1952, transposed into the first person, and inserted into *Junkie*, the second half corresponding to pages 1–4 here.

MCR MS.

Ten-page typescript, mailed to Ginsberg August 1953, of the text that was edited down and entitled "Mexico City Return" when added to *Queer* in 1985. The most complete copy is in the Ginsberg Collection at Columbia; some carbons also in the Ginsberg Papers at Stanford (Correspondence Series 3, Box 59.1, Folder 12).

1. "a Jewish boy named Carl Steinberg": "Jewish" is an autograph insert on page 3 of the first Q ms. (Berg), a typed insert on the first Q ms. (Stanford carbon), and was incorporated into the third Q ms. On page 3 of the first Q ms. the name is spelled "Karl," but on pages 4–5 it changes to "Carl," as regularized for the 1985 edition.

1. "The first time he saw Carl, Lee thought": immediately before this line, the first Q ms. (3) has a sentence canceled in autograph: **"Since Lee had been on the junk during this time he had made no attempt to get to know Karl better on the chance he might prove {turn out} available."** Immediately after the line, there is another sentence canceled in type: **"There is something I would like if I hadn't pawned my balls for junk. Alt—If I hadn't checked it with the junk man / alt. If I hadn't checked the family jewels at the junk counter."**

3. "can't use it, don't need it, don't want it": canceled in autograph on the first Q ms. (4) and omitted in the third Q ms., these phrases were restored for the 1985 edition. Note:

"sorry," not canceled in the first Q ms., has been restored for this edition.

3. "A television set. . . .": this sentence has been changed to restore the syntax of the original, and the phrase "like a Frankenstein monster," which was omitted for the 1985 edition, has been restored in place of "the final touch of unpleasantness," which was canceled in autograph on the first Q ms. (5) and omitted from the third Q ms.

5. "His face showed" to "pantry shelf": for an early version of these lines, see Burroughs' letter to Kerouac, April 1952, in *The Letters of William S. Burroughs, 1945–1959*, edited by Oliver Harris (New York: Viking, 1993), 114.

5. "to take advantage of any weakness in another": the first Q ms. (6) has two phrases canceled in autograph: **"sign of"** before "weakness," and **"his opponent, and everyone else was his opponent"** before the insertion of "another." The lines closely echo F. Scott Fitzgerald's "A Short Trip Home"; see also note in *Letters*, 114.

7. "Lee was deeply hurt": at this point the first Q ms. (8) has, canceled in autograph, a slightly different version of lines redrafted on ms. page 49, and which appear here on page 50 ("In any relation of love" to "shock and disbelief").

8. "not ready yet to go home": at this point the first Q ms. (9) continues with ten pages (from "He was in a cheap cantina" to "He stayed off the junk"), which conclude the original chapter 1 of "Queer." This material was lightly edited and transposed into the first person to form pages 13–24 of the thirty-eight-page insert Burroughs added in July 1952 to his "Junk" manuscript (in *Junky*, 107–16; see notes on pages 163–64 for the key deletions Burroughs made when transposing this material). One of the unused passages (from "Scenes from the chaotic, drunken month" to "malicious bitch smile"; first Q ms., 17–18), which would have appeared after "darkening room" in *Junky* (115), was inserted in *Queer* for the 1985 edition (see page 53 in this edition and note below).

10. "but *he* is going to heaven": at this point a variant, and probably earlier, draft manuscript page (Stanford), which over-
laps the first Q ms. pages 19–20, continues: **"I guess the
padre gave him a pep talk. Did I ever tell you about my
friend Dubois? He told me this in all seriousness[;] you
know how a sensitive young writer lost his faith[?] It
seems he went to confess mutual masturbation with
another boy and the priest said[,] 'And how big was this
other boy's thing[,] my son?' Joe laughed the open
friendly laugh that made him universally liked. 'I think
you did tell me that before but it bears repeating,' he
said. 'Well the little bastard Hector is as queer as I
am. . . .'"** Note: "Hector" is changed to "Maurice" in the
first Q ms.

13. "He was sick" to "glow in the dark": for an early version of
these lines, see Burroughs' letter to Kerouac, April 1952
(*Letters*, 114).

13. "Eugene Allerton": in the first Q ms. (22) the first name is an
autograph insert in Alan Ansen's hand, and so made in fall
1953 when Ansen assisted Burroughs with his manuscript
prior to retyping.

13. "exotic and Oriental": in the first Q ms. (22) the phrase is
followed by **"like a temple dancer,"** canceled in autograph.
Note the recurrence of this phrase in the Chimu Bar scene.

15. "his departure was abrupt": at this point the first Q ms. (23)
continues with material (from "Some people you can spot"
to "twisted with hate") that would be transposed into the
first person and added to "Junk" (in *Junky*, 117–19). The
only omission was the very first line of the first Q ms. material (i.e., before "Some people"): **"He turned off Coahuila
into the block where he lived, and spotted Old Joe a
block away."**

15. "leer of naked lust, wrenched": the title *Naked Lunch* was
coined by Kerouac in fall 1953, on hearing Ginsberg mis-

reading out loud Burroughs' mistyping of these phrases in the first Q ms. (26). Note that in the previous sentence, "ghastly" is a typed insert for the canceled **"unfortunate."**

16. "The Chimu Bar looks like any cantina": from here to "shaking hands" on page 18 has been restored for this edition. This material, which appears in the first Q ms. (27–28), was lightly edited and transposed into the first person to add to "Junk" (in *Junky*, 93–94). Due to the omission of this section, the 1985 edition added a bridging sentence: "He took a cab to the Chimu Bar, which was a fag bar frequented by Mexicans, and spent the night with a young boy he met there."

17. "Though he was near forty. . . .": Burroughs quotes this line in his letter to Ginsberg of April 5, 1952 (*Letters*, 111).

18. "Lee's body was moving": from here to "relaxed away from the other's body" were lines omitted when this material was transposed from "Queer" to add to "Junk."

21. "on the surface": restores phrasing from the first Q ms. (30).

25. "Allerton was intelligent. . . .": restores a line lightly canceled on the first Q ms. (38).

35. "*homosexual*. I was a homosexual": restores the repetition in the first Q ms. (39).

36. "slupping sound" and "ghastly slup": restores original spelling from first Q ms. (40). See note 25 on page xlix.

37. "of Communism I mean, of course": the first Q ms. (41) continues with a further line, canceled in autograph: **"I saw that no good could come my way from a movement that suggests/proposes, even insincerely, compulsory labor for all."**

43. "a drug he called Telepathine": the first Q ms. (45) continues with a phrase canceled in autograph: **"so-called by him, that is."**

44. "a charge of anti-Semitism": the first Q ms. (46) continues with a sentence canceled in autograph: **"I recall a friend of mine was putting up a Jewish refugee in his house and the refugee continually accused him of anti-Semitism."**

47. "I hear Jim Cochan" to "hard to catch" (48): added for the 1985 edition. From "Thank God" to "unappetizing person" derives from Burroughs' April 1952 letter to Kerouac, and from "who is said to play" to "ugly as people get" derives from Burroughs' June 4, 1952, letter to Ginsberg (*Letters*, 114–15, 130).

53. "Scenes from the chaotic" to "malicious bitch smile": these lines were inserted at this point for the 1985 edition from the first Q ms. (17–18), where they were canceled in autograph (see note for page 8). The phrase "His childhood friend" was added for the 1985 edition, as was the final sentence ("The faces blended . . .").

59. "an Abyssinian prince": the first Q ms. (55) continues with a line canceled in type: **"Came near getting a camel iron up my ass trying to move that critter at a camel auction."**

60. "The routine" to "the night": added for the 1985 edition.

66. "They left by bus" to "sensible and calm": added for the 1985 edition.

67. "Lee was reading aloud" to "yacking falsetto" (68): under the heading "Reconstruction of lost Panama Chapter," this material was written by Burroughs in 1985 and, with very light editing, has been inserted here to precede the final page of the "Panama Chapter" (see note below).

68. "Want to pick up" to "in regard to that fifty dollars" (69): this passage from the first Q ms. (62) restores the last half page of the three-page "Panama Chapter"; discovered in the William Burroughs Papers at the Berg Collection in 2009.

71. "in a tiny plane which had to struggle": added for the 1985 edition.

74. "How the fuck should I know?": the first Q ms. (64) continues with a line not used for the 1985 edition: **"They ate in a dark restaurant that had curtained booths."**

78. "Lee looked at the boy and thought": the 1985 edition has "said in English," which is canceled in pencil on the first Q ms. (67), with "thought" an autograph insert.

79. "Lee could see the boat" to "happy times": restores lines in the first Q ms. (68) not used for the 1985 edition. The insert includes two editorial revisions ("could see" for "saw" and "Gene" for "Jean") and two elements canceled in autograph on the ms. ("smoking weed with Gene [*sic*]" and "He lay down with his head in Allerton's lap").

80. "you say, 'Yage!'": the first words were an addition made for the 1985 edition. Note that Stanford has a fragment with the draft line: **"The Yage removes anything I don't like in someone etc. 'But you'll be so much <u>nicer</u> after I tidy you up.'"**

80. "Horrible stuff": for a version of this account of taking peyote, see Burroughs' letter to Ginsberg of June 4, 1952 (*Letters*, 130), passages in *Junky* (122–23), and Kerouac's letters of June 3 and 5, 1952, in Jack Kerouac, *Selected Letters, 1940–1956*, edited by Ann Charters (New York: Viking, 1995), 362–71.

81. "Another dream I had a chlorophyll habit": this is an autograph insert on the first Q ms. (69), replacing a line canceled in autograph: **"Another routine I was hung up on chlorophyll."**

81. "Stick out your tongue": on the first Q ms. (69) this line is canceled in pencil and an alternative written in: **"Open your mouth."**

81. "That is the Russian dream, and America is not far behind": the final phrase is an autograph insert on the first Q ms. (69),

revising the original: **"That is the Russian dream. The American dream."**

81. "on the beach": an autograph insert on the first Q ms. (69); the phrase replaced the words **"here and rest and soak up the sun,"** (canceled in autograph).

83. "Guayaquil is built" to "happy and gay. Lee walked on" (85): this material appears in the first Q ms. (75–77) and was moved here, out of sequence, for the 1985 edition. In the first Q ms. (71), this chapter (numbered 11) begins with the passage that starts, "Six or seven boys . . . ," and which appears on page 85 in this edition.

83. "shades the stone benches": the first Q ms. (75) continues with a phrase canceled in autograph: **"and provides an infinite number of places to sit pleasantly."**

84. "An iron bedstead painted light pink": the first Q ms. (76) continues with two phrases: **"a chair, a pair of socks,"** canceled in autograph, and **"Odds and ends of lives,"** canceled in type. In the following sentence Lee is cut off **"by the glass wall of an aquarium,"** another phrase canceled in autograph.

84. "Lee's wet-dream country": this phrase, restored from the first Q ms. (76), was canceled in autograph on the ms., replacing the phrase, canceled in type, **"dream of unbridled sex."**

85. "A slight, involuntary sound of pain. . . .": this line was canceled in a mix of type and autograph on the first Q ms. (77), as was a preceding typed insert: **"The cry of a tormented animal that does not understand the re[ason]."**

87. "He licked his lips" to "all kinds of ": these lines, at the lower margin of the first Q ms. (71), were unintentionally omitted in the transcription for the 1985 edition.

87. "so queer it rocked you": added for the 1985 edition.

87. "The statue was on" to "was a stone bench": these lines in the first Q ms. (72), lightly canceled in autograph, have been restored and moved so that they appear before rather than after the line "Lee stood looking at the statue."

88. "The pension where they were staying. . . .": this line on the first Q ms. (72), a barely legible autograph insert on the margin of the page, has been restored.

90. "The food was terrible" to "being prepared": in the first Q ms. (75) these lines follow "'Let's hit the sack,' said Allerton, 'I'm tired'" and precede "Guayaquil is built along a river" (pages 95 and 83, respectively, in this edition). They were moved for the 1985 edition to follow "Las Playas was . . . a dreary middle-class resort" (page 91 in this edition). They have been inserted here instead, since they describe the pension in Guayaquil rather than Las Playas.

90. "I'd like to dig" to "sort of thing": this line, a barely legible autograph insert on the margin of the first Q ms. (75), has been restored.

90. "Straight from Dickens": line restored from the first Q ms. (77).

90. "dropped a dead fish on his desk": the 1985 edition has "lobster," which was canceled in autograph on the first Q ms. (77), with "fish" inserted. At this point the ms. continues with a version of the following lines canceled in autograph: **"Well, really I don't know why you tell me about it. You must realize how distasteful this sort of thing is. I should think you might show some consideration. After all, it's rather disgusting to see someone grovelling about the embassy."**

92. "The water was shockingly cold": restored from the first Q ms. (79) and moved to the end of this paragraph, the sentence order of which was rearranged for the 1985 edition.

93. "is classically simple and": restores a phrase canceled in autograph on the first Q ms. (74).

97. "Springs, moss" to "lawn-mower whine": added for the 1985 edition.

97. "They stopped" to "stink of its cage" (98): added for the 1985 edition.

98. "The view" to "phantom bus outside": except for two sentence fragments ("the snow-covered . . . high Andes," and "Lee and Allerton . . . brandy"), this paragraph was added for the 1985 edition.

98. "as they descended into the lush green valley": this phrase was added for the 1985 edition, along with some minor corrections to this paragraph.

99. "and found a room" to "asleep at once": added for the 1985 edition.

99. "He wanted to start a head-shrinking plant to put the deal on mass-production basis": restores phrases canceled in autograph on the first Q ms. (80) and reattributes speech to Lee, rather than Morgan.

99. "Lee nodded, without saying anything": added for the 1985 edition.

100. "We can hardly pretend" to "Doctor Cotter, I presume": this sequence comes after "It will take you about three hours more" (page 102 in this edition) in the first Q ms. (81–82) and was moved here for the 1985 edition.

100. "We are lucky to hit him in that condition" to "sucres' worth of Yage": in the first Q ms. (82) these lines are autograph inserts that replace the canceled lines **The Dutchman told me Cotter was starving. I prefer a man broke when I want something from him. Easier to interest him in the deal if he is flat."**

102. "*quebradas*": in the first Q ms. (82) the term is given as "Quebrados," and for the 1985 edition it was changed to "*quebrajas.*" While both terms translate as "fissure" or "ravine," I have restored Burroughs' original, following the example of

Henri Michaux in his 1929 *Ecuador: A Travel Journal,* translated by Robin Magowan (Chicago: Northwestern University Press, 2001), which refers to hundred-feet-deep *quebradas* in Quito (66).

105. "Cotter was supposedly trying" to "and start biting" (106): added for the 1985 edition.

109. "Two Years Later": "Epilogue" in the 1985 edition. The ten-page, August 1953 typescript from which this material derives began with lines that mostly appeared as part of the July 8, 1953, letter in *The Yage Letters* (48–49, from "Lima cold, damp and depressing" to "Suddenly I have to leave right now"; see also notes on page 122), followed by material that approximates the opening pages of the typescript's original notebook source; see from "A bus called Proletario" to "'Lobsters cooked in whisky'" in Oliver Harris, *Everything Lost: The Latin American Notebook of William S. Burroughs* (Columbus: Ohio State University Press, 2008), 107–8.

110. "I finally caught him . . .": this sentence, and the following two, have been restructured according to the MCR ms. (2) and, in the case of the phrasing "Such languid animal grace," to the notebook original (*Everything Lost,* 110–11).

110. "Many so-called" to "intensity of pursuit": these lines, which followed "ambiguous gesture of hostility" in the 1985 edition, have been restored to their original position in the MCR ms. for this edition. The line, "They think it can capture their soul and take it away" has been restored from page 2 of the MCR ms., with "can" replacing "could" as per a correction on the Stanford "Yage" ms. (33).

111. "'Your Cheatin' Heart'": the MCR ms. (3) continues: **"Such crap as that."**

111. "autonomous insect life": the MCR ms. (3) continues: **"What a distasteful sight!"**

112. "with his mouth open": the MCR ms. (3) continues: **"Pist, Jack. I gotta boat load of irradiated girls from**

Hirosheema [*sic*]. Just off the boat. Hot as a plutonium pile."

112. "making money": both "Yage" mss. (Stanford and Berg) show this correction, in autograph and type, respectively, from "losing money" in the MCR ms. (which was used for the 1985 edition).

112. "Flew up to Tapachula" to "twenty centavos" (113): these lines have been restored from the MCR ms. (4). Preceding this passage, the manuscript has more description of Panama and, briefly, Guatemala City. None of this concerns Allerton, although the Stanford "Yage" ms., which uses this material for the "July 13 Panama" letter, concludes with these lines: "Flying back to Mexico with stopover in Guatemala City. I never heard from Allerton after I left Mexico, and I want to find out where he is and why he hasn't written. As Ever, Bill."

113. "Dream about Allerton" to "find out why": these lines have been restored from the MCR ms. (5).

114. "Easy now. Cool. Cool": restored from the MCR ms. (6). Note that in the previous sentence the ms. has "Tato's," changed in autograph to "Lola's."

114. "Pepe behind the bar": on the Stanford copy of the MCR ms. (6) this is changed to "Louie" (which is how the name is given in the Berg "Yage" ms.); for the 1985 edition the phrase "the same old bartender" was substituted.

115. "A wave of pain . . .": this sentence has been restored from the MCR ms. (7). Note: in the original notebook draft of this material, the following line is, "Then I knew I was hung up on M. [i.e., Marker] just the same as ever" (*Everything Lost*, 144–45).

115. "He must have gotten" to "Why?" and "the pain inside" to "wound" (116): restored from the MCR ms. (7).

116. "I could feel the pain ease up a bit": restored from the MCR ms. (7).

116. "He said something" to "home address" (117): restored from the MCR ms. (8).

117. "so much aging tissue": the MCR ms. (8) continues: **"The citizens of Panama obviously stem from a long line of pimps. They are quite simply a low subhuman form of life."**

117. "Dream that night" to "same currency": restored from the MCR ms. (8).

117. "That night I dreamed I finally found Allerton": added for the 1985 edition, replacing **"Thought up gag for if I find Allerton"** in the Columbia original of the MCR ms. (8); on Stanford's copy "gag" is corrected in autograph to **"this routine."** The word "someplace," in both mss., has been retained here instead of the 1985 addition "in some Central American backwater." The next two sentences ("He seemed surprised" to "missing persons") were also added in 1985.

117. "Haven't you forgotten something, Gene?": on the MCR ms. (8) the name is, typically, spelled "Jean," but in the original draft in his notebook Burroughs uses first "Bill" and then "Louie" (*Everything Lost*, 114–17).

118. "electron microscope": in all mss. this is "electric microscope."

118. "Not when the old Skip Tracer goes out on a job": at this point there is an important typed aside on the MCR ms. (9): **"Shift of tempo. This was written three days later while I was drinking a cupa tea inna quick lunch joint. Like taking dictation. I have less and less control over what I write."** Note that on the Stanford copy the last three words are canceled and replaced, in Burroughs' hand, by **"my routines."**

118. "The Skip Tracer's face goes blank and dreamy": from this point to the end, the tense was changed from present to past for the 1985 edition; it has been restored to present for this edition.

119. "inside the window": restored from the MCR ms. (10); the 1985 edition substituted the phrase "over a sofa."